Bina Lobell's Super Secret Diary

Ruchama Feuerman

JUDAICA
PRESS

For my wonderful children

Bina Lobell's Super-Secret Diary
© 2014 Ruchama Feuerman

ISBN: 978-1-60763-154-5

Editor: Bracha Steinberg
Proofreader: Hadassa Goldsmith
Illustrations: Evgeniy Ognarov
Cover and internal design and layout: Nachum Shapiro

The Judaica Press, Inc.
123 Ditmas Avenue / Brooklyn, NY 11218
718-972-6200 / 800-972-6201
info@judaicapress.com
www.judaicapress.com

Manufactured in China

MONDAY

I go to a school that has just a few kids my age.
There's five of us, because it's a homeschool. That
means school happens at home. The only thing is,
it's not at my home. It's at Deena's home.

Other kids are always asking me why I go to a
homeschool. And I don't know what to say. That's
my big problem. I never know what to answer when
they ask me Those Kinds of Questions. You know
what I mean? Like "Why do you have freckles on
your ears?" Or "How come your parents don't fix
that big dent in their car?" Or "Didn't you wear

those socks yesterday ... and the day before?"

By the time I figure out what to answer back, it's already a week later.

Or sometimes I don't know what to say, even to myself. Like, for instance, my next-door neighbor Shaindy goes to a regular school. Just yesterday she asked me, "Bina, what grade are you in?" That's my name, by the way.

The strange thing is, I can't say, because my homeschool doesn't have any real grades. It's all a big mishmash - third, fourth, and fifth grades all lumped together in one room with yellow walls. So I just stood there and pretended to be very interested in my fingernail, which had a little piece of dirt under it.

But now that I think about it, I'm nine, so I guess that makes me a fourth grader.

You know what? Next time Shaindy asks me, I'll just

say fourth grade. That's right.

My teacher, Morah Zeldy, gave us our own notebooks. She said it's good for writing down what we're thinking. She also said it's good to ask one question at the end of the day.

Question for the day: Why do people have to ask me so many boring questions?

TUESDAY
Let me tell you about my school.

I told you it's in Deena's house, right? Her house looks like a farmhouse. It has lots of wood and windows big as doors, with tons of sunlight pouring in so you never need to turn on the lights. Except on cloudy days.

We get to use the kitchen to make food. The cool thing about the kitchen is that part of it was made to fit our size. Even Miri, the youngest of us, can reach the faucets. The dishes aren't humongous like for an adult, but are perfect for kids. We make our sandwiches at school, and sometimes soup for lunch and challahs for Shabbos and muffins for snack. That's the good part. But we can't use any sugar in the muffins or cakes. That's another thing this school is really strict about - gotta be healthy! I dunno. Will eating a teeny bit of sugar really wreck your whole body?

Also, you won't find any peanuts in this school. That's because I'm allergic to them. Really, really allergic. Like, my throat squeezes shut and my breathing stops, I break out in gross red patches everywhere, and I faint. I think my eyes roll back in my head, too, but since I can't actually see my eyes, I can't tell you for sure. That's why I have to carry an EpiPen around with me everywhere. It saved my life two times already.

Well, so what if I can't eat peanut butter. I bet you I wouldn't even like it. It's probably like eating brown glue with a peanut flavor. It gets stuck between

your teeth and looks yucky. But I sure wish we
could have all the junk food parties they have in
regular schools. Those salty Bissli crunchy things
from Israel, and Milk Munches, and lollipops as big as
grapefruits, and those hard, chewy Laffy Taffies,
and Jolly Ranchers, and the green, pink, and blue
Candy Planets that are so gushy mushy that I can't
stop eating them ...

I always ask Morah Zeldy how come all the other
kids in the other schools eat junk food and they
look the same healthy as us.

She just says, "You'll see the difference when you
get older."

I sure hope so, because otherwise I've been
suffering for no reason. Though I have to tell you,
Morah Zeldy looks like the healthiest grown-up I
ever met. She has pink cheeks and her eyes shine
like blue marbles. But even if I eat a bucketful of
blueberries, my brown eyes will never be blue like
hers. Though somebody said her cousin drinks tons

of carrot juice and now her skin looks orangey.

Morah Zeldy has like ten outfits that she wears.
On Mondays, it's a blue outfit with fat buttons.
On Tuesdays, it's a black skirt with a beige top. On
Wednesdays, it's a dark green skirt with these
cute pleats on the bottom and a pale yellow top.
You get the idea. After the two weeks are up, she
goes back to the blue outfit with the fat buttons.
That is probably my favorite outfit. Deena likes the
green skirt best, though.

Question for the day: If eating tons of carrots
turns your skin orange, then why doesn't eating
tons of blueberries turn your eyes blue?

WEDNESDAY

Shaindy, my next-door neighbor, just said to me yesterday, "You're so lucky. There's only five girls in your whole school, so I bet you're all best friends, right?" And I just nodded and said, "Right," because I don't want to say lashon hara. Also, I don't want her to feel sorry for me. Because the truth is, I have no close friends except for one girl - Deena.

Deena has brown hair with lots of red lights in them. My hair is brown, too, but so far I can't find any red lights. The homeschool is in her house. We learn together, we play jump rope together, we catch ladybugs together, and we have play dates together on Shabbos. The only thing is, it's no fun going to her house for play dates, because then it feels like school.

Actually - and I don't tell anyone this - I like school. I like my teacher, Morah Zeldy. She teaches us Torah, and math and reading, too. We take nature walks and we learn all the names of the plants and flowers. Once we made an oven out of bricks in the backyard and sometimes we even bake on it! We

do all these different, creative things because our
school is something called Monty Sorry. I think that
means "creative." We're always going on class trips.
My favorite is on Rosh Chodesh, when she takes us
to meet a tzaddekes - a really, really good person.

Last week we went to see Rebbetzin Kugler.
Miri - she's eight, the youngest in our school -
asked the rebbetzin, "Are you a real tzaddekes?
Like from a book?"

I wondered how the rebbetzin was going to answer
that one. I mean, what's she supposed to say? Yes, I
am! I am such a good person!

The rebbetzin just laughed and said, "Me? My
goodness, we're all tzaddekeses in training!" Which
kinda made me think the whole ride home. So maybe
it wasn't such a silly question after all.

Guess what? I like davening, especially on the days
we sing the words and say them real slow, and
when I close my eyes, I feel like a bird's carrying my

words up to Hashem. That's how we daven in my school. Sometimes.

But here's my real problem. I need Deena, for everything. To be my friend, to help me out in class, for play dates, and to stick up for me. The problem is, she acts like she can tell me what to do. You know, boss me all the time.

I was playing with some school play dough and Deena said, "You can't do that. You're making crumbs all over the floor! Stop it right now."

So I stopped playing with the play dough. But why didn't she tell any of the other kids to stop? You know why? Because she thinks she can get away with it.

And she can.

Just as I was going to sleep, I thought, Why didn't I say, "Deena Berman, you're not the boss of my hands"? Or maybe I should've said, "If it was against the rules, Morah Zeldy would've said so!"

Yeah.

Question for the day: Can a kid <u>become</u> a "boss-in-training," or are you just born that way?

THURSDAY

I have a secret to tell. It's not one of those nice secrets like somebody's getting engaged or someone's planning a surprise birthday party for me.

Here's the thing. I get angry. Really, really angry.
The whole day I'm good at school and act nice
to everybody, but when I get home, if something
bothers me - watch out.

Like today when my little brother threw some
of my stamps into the toilet. He's just three. He
thought he did me a favor. "Look, Bina. It's pretty
colors in the toilet!"

I ran over. I saw one stamp from Belgium and one
from France. The third, I couldn't see. My beautiful
precious stamps! I felt my whole face turning red
like I'd eaten a peanut and was having an attack.
Levi just turned to me with a curious look on his
face.

I pushed him. Hard. Then I started to scream and
shout at the top of my lungs.

Ima came running up the stairs. Her hands were full
of dough. She was in the middle of baking challah.
"What happened? Did someone get hurt?" Her eyes

were darting all over the room with this scared
look. Levi was crying.

I just pointed, teary-eyed, at the toilet. "Look what
Levi did!"

She looked into the toilet and then stared hard
at me. "For that you screamed like a banshee? I
almost had a heart attack!"

She hugged Levi and said to him, "Your sister has to
learn to control her temper."

I felt so angry I stomped off into my bedroom.
Then I took out my notebook.

Okay. Time out. I'm writing a poem.

SOMETIMES I'M BAD
Sometimes I'm bad.
Sometimes I'm good.
Sometimes I'm just plain me.

But sometimes I'm as bad as an elephant's
tantrum.
Bad it is
And worse it will be.
The anger is fire starting in my toes
Rising up my stomach and coming out through
my nose.
It's stronger than a bomb crashing a town
Kicking like a person running in a race
Punching like a prisoner trying to get out of jail.
That is how I am when I'm bad.
My little brother looks at me like I'm a lion about
to eat him up.
Ima is shocked.
Her nose puffs out, her face turns red.
Her eyebrows go down like slanting slides.
And that's when I see -
How did this happen?
My mother is now as angry as me.

I feel a little better now that I wrote down my
poem. I hope tomorrow I don't get so mad at
anybody. The truth is, I don't get angry and hit

people all the time. Only sometimes. Now and then. But that's no good, either. Because – I just realized. I'm a tzaddekes-in-training!

Question for the day: What would it look like if an elephant had a tantrum?

SUNDAY

Malka – she's my kid sister, if I didn't tell you already. She is tons of fun, and has red hair, and we always put on shows together with our dolls – but guess what?

She goes to a regular school! Every morning she puts on her light blue oxford top and her dark blue Bnos Devora skirt, and she fixes her hair in a ponytail, and I watch her go off. Ima always says I'm the lucky one, and Malka stomps her feet most mornings and says she wants to be homeschooled just like me, and not have to do homework and wear the same scratchy outfit every day.

But you know what? If Ima thinks homeschool is so great, then Malka should be going, too, just like me, but Ima and Abba explained that sometimes it's better for sisters to be separated. And there isn't another homeschool for Malka to go to. So I'm the lucky one. I guess.

But if we both were homeschooled, we'd be able to play together all the time.

Even though she's only six, she's already had a gazillion play dates. Chaya Esther, Rivky, Shana, Elisheva, Nechama. I can't believe it. And that makes things harder for me.

Let me tell you what happened today. Shaindy - she's my next-door neighbor (wait, did I already tell you that thirty-eight times?) - well, we were playing together, making Sukkos decorations in my house. I was so happy, because she usually doesn't have time for play dates during the week or on Sundays, either.

So Ima put out slices of pears. I took a slice and made a bracha.

Shaindy looked at the fruit all squinty-eyed. "My mother never makes me eat fruit."

"My mother doesn't make me," I told her. "I like pears." But Shaindy just had this ew-look on her face like she was smelling old socks.

Then she said, "Could you show me your needle?" She sat up in her chair and looked all hopeful and bright-eyed at me.

I was about to say, What needle? But then I

remembered: my EpiPen. I stared at her. "How do you know about my EpiPen?"

"My mother told me. You have a peanut allergy."

So I showed her my needle. I keep it in my knapsack. I told her how I take it everywhere with me. I explained how I stick it into my leg like I'm a doctor giving myself a shot. The good thing is, now I'm not scared of getting shots like most kids are.

"You're brave," she said. She shook her head and her curls went boing all over the place. "I could never do that."

That made me feel sort of good, like I'm strong, and sort of bad, like I have a hard life. But Abba always says to focus on the good, so that's what I did.

Then we each made a picture of the seven special fruits of Israel. Her pomegranate looked like a squashed apple and her dates sort of looked like roaches, but I didn't say anything.

Then she started cutting construction paper to make a paper chain while I drew a picture of two doves. I made my doves hold a piece of white cloth in their beaks, like a tallis, and I wrote the words from the davening, "Spread your sukkah of peace over us."

It gave me such a good cozy feeling inside, because that's what a sukkah is, a place of shalom. My mother likes to call it the Happiness Box, because you should try to only have happy feelings inside the sukkah. She says, "If you want to whine, you can do that outside the sukkah."

So I was drawing my letters, making them look straight and pretty, when Shaindy turned and looked at my picture. "That's weird," she said.

"What's weird?" I asked.

"What are you drawing birds for? Nobody puts that kind of picture in a sukkah."

I looked at my drawing. She was right. I never saw
this kind of decoration in a sukkah before. I felt so
bad, I stopped drawing.

"What kind of decorations do you put up?" I finally
asked.

"Oh," her eyes looked up and faraway, "you know,
paper chains, and those shiny things that twirl
around, and pictures of lulavs and esrogs, and
pictures of Yerushalayim. Those kinds of things."
She nodded importantly, and her curls boinged
against her shoulders again.

I stared at my picture. I could see what she meant.
It did look a little weird. I wanted to crumple it into a
ball, but before I could do anything, Shaindy jumped
up. She clapped her hand to her forehead.

"I can't believe how late it is - gotta go!"

"What's happening?"

"I made a play date with somebody," she said. "I almost forgot."

She gathered up her pomegranate blob picture and her paper chain. "See you later!" she said and ran out the door. But I thought you were having a play date with me, I almost said.

Whatever.

Shaindy's lucky. She's got twenty-four girls to choose from for play dates. I can't even imagine ten girls in one class. That would be huge. My sister Malka is so lucky.

I looked down at my drawing. Shaindy was right. The doves didn't look good. They looked like white chickens. Or rabbits. Ima came up from the basement holding a basket of laundry. She tries to do all the laundry on Sunday, because she works during the week as a court stenographer. She once explained what that is exactly, but I still can't figure it out. Something about judges and typing.

"What happened to Shaindy?" she asked.

"She had a play date," I said, not looking at her. I started cleaning up all the pieces of construction paper scattered on the table. Leftovers from the paper chain.

Ima said nothing. Her mouth was twisting in that way it gets when she's annoyed, but she still wouldn't say a word of lashon hara. Then she glanced down at my picture. She set down her basket of laundry and picked up the picture. She read the letters. "U'fros aleinu sukkas shlo-" Spread your sukkah of -

"Shlomecha," I finished. I still had three letters to do. "Your peace."

"Did you come up with this idea on your own?" Ima asked me quietly.

"I just thought of it."

"Bina, it's ..." - she closed her eyes tight and got that davening look on her face - "beautiful! Amaaaazing. It captures what Sukkos is all about. I want to laminate this." She stood there, hugging my picture to her, but not too hard; otherwise she'd ruin it.

Then she said, "You have such a special way of looking at the world. This is so ... original."

The way she said it made me feel so good inside. Then I said, "Ima, what's 'orange-al'?"

"Original," she corrected. She squinted, one eye shut. "I guess that's when you're not a copycat, when you're," she paused, thinking, "when you make something or say something that's never been said before. Or maybe ... when you're just being yourself."

That didn't make much sense to me. Because who would I be if I'm not me - Shaindy?

Later that day, we really did go to a store and get my doves laminated. It turned out to be the best day. I'm glad I'm 'orange-al' - whatever that means.

But just before I went to sleep, I thought, I'd rather have Shaindy as a friend.

Question for the day: Does Hashem want me to be the same as everyone else?

TWO WEEKS LATER, WEDNESDAY

Sorry, Diary, that I couldn't write in you for a long time.

First it was Yom Kippur. Then it was Sukkos. Then it was Chol HaMoed vacation and we went to the zoo, and a jungle safari, and eight monkeys climbed all over our car! That was the best part, but Abba didn't think so. His car now has monkey scratches.

Then on the fourth night of Chol HaMoed, Deena and her whole family came over for a meal. That felt good, too, because I'm always going over to Deena's house, but this time her whole family came to mine. Well, to my sukkah. Our mothers are, like, best friends.

I love our sukkah. We painted pictures of Yerushalayim straight onto the walls, so this way, no matter how hard it rains or how hard the wind blows, most of the decorations won't fall down. And my father hangs up lots of pine branches, so

that our whole sukkah smells like a forest or air
freshener, but the good kind.

Only thing is, while Deena and her family were over,
the pine needles kept falling into my butternut
squash soup. I tried to take them out without
anybody noticing, but then Levi had to shout at me,
"Don't put those green bugs next to my plate!" And
then suddenly nobody wanted to finish their soup.
Poor Ima.

Deena's mother coughed and tried to change the
subject. She pointed to my picture of the doves.
"Look how beautiful that decoration is!" she said in
an excited voice. "Look how creative!"

Deena's mother loves creative stuff. That's why
she started the homeschool. She thinks regular
schools take away kids' love of learning. She even
trained to be a Monty Sorry teacher, but now
she's just, like, the director of the school, and lets
Morah Zeldy do the teaching.

But maybe Deena's mother shouldn't have complimented my picture so much. Because then all the adults jumped in and said how special it was, and next thing you know, I saw this frown squiggle come between Deena's eyebrows. I knew what that frown squiggle meant because I'd seen it before. It meant that Deena wanted compliments, too. Not a good sign.

A minute later Deena let out a humongous yawn in the middle of Abba's amazing Sukkah ghost story. So my mother said, "Why don't you two go inside and play?"

I really wanted to hear the rest of the story, but I went in and let Deena play with all my dolls, even with Jennie, my Fake American Girl Doll Who Looks Really Real. The good thing about Deena is that she's fun. She's great for all kinds of games and putting on pretend shows. She's not the type to say, ew, you're eating a pear, or to speak in a prissy voice, and say, that's gross, if you suddenly burp by accident. And she won't scream if some mud

falls on the side of her shoe. She'll just wipe it off.
That's the good side.

After we put on this whole show with my dolls,
Deena had to sort of ruin it though by saying, "I'm
getting a real American Girl Doll for my birthday."

"My father says it's a waste of money and you
can't tell the difference," I shot back.

"Oh, I can," said Deena in her know-it-all voice, the
voice that says I'm the smartest nine-year-old on
the planet. GRRRR!!

"Can't you see how phony her neck is?" She pointed.

I covered poor Jennie's ears. I know she's just a doll,
but I always feel like I got punched in the stomach
when anybody insults Jennie.

Deena went on, "But she has really nice hair," and
I forgave Deena right away. "Look," she said, "it's
reddish a little, like mine."

That's true. It was practically the same color.

"Hey, let's make a different hairstyle for Jennie," Deena said.

I said no, because last time Deena did that, Jennie's hair got messed up really bad. It looked like poor Jennie had gotten electrocuted.

"You have to let me, because I'm the guest," Deena said. "Hachnasas orchim," she said in that know-it-all voice of hers.

So I let her change the hairstyle and braid her hair
real tight, and now, a week later, Jennie looks like
a yard full of weeds, or a haystack, or maybe just
a scary witch. Boy, am I dumb for letting her braid
Jennie's hair. Or maybe it was a mitzvah to let her.
Isn't it good to be mevater - to give in?

Just last night I asked my father, "Do I have to lend
something to somebody if I know they're going to
ruin it?"

My father frowned. "You should try to get her
interested in something else."

"What if that doesn't work? What if she's real,
you know ..." - I tried to think of the right way to
describe Deena - "... stubborn?"

"You can say no. It's all right to say, 'No, now's not a
good time to play with the doll.'"

My eyes opened wide. "How did you know I was
talking about my doll?"

He gave me a funny smile.

"But Abba, I did say that, and you know what she said?" I frowned, remembering the whole conversation. "She said, 'I'm the guest. You have to let me do what I want.'"

"Tell her, guests don't remind you they're guests." Then he walked out fast to go to shul. (I think I sometimes drive him a little crazy.)

Question for the day: How come nightgowns for American Girl Dolls cost more than my own nightgowns?

SUNDAY

Today Abba took down the sukkah. First I helped put away all the sukkah decorations. I made sure not to let my laminated dove picture get crinkled. I used a little screwdriver to get all the thumbtacks out, but then Levi threw them all over the floor.

"Snow!" he shouted. "It's snowing."

"Don't do that!" I said.

"I want to!" He threw a bunch of tacks at my arm.
Lucky I was wearing a jacket, but I yelled "Ouch!"
just to get him in trouble. But Ima and Abba
weren't even there to give him that better-stop-
right-now look.

So I gave him my own look and said, "Do you want to
step on the thumbtacks and get them stuck inside
your foot?"

His eyes turned big and happy. "Like a robot?" he
said excitedly.

"No, like it hurts real bad and then you might have
to get a shot with a really long needle and you'll feel
stiff and sore for days afterward."

Levi said nothing. He just stuck his thumb in his
mouth and sat on a bench with a kind of scared
look on his face. At least he wasn't throwing the
thumbtacks everywhere.

Later, I took down Levi's yellow esrog picture - it looked like an egg yolk, but I didn't tell him, and he started to scream, "No, I want it up. Up!" He pointed at the sukkah panels and began to cry.

Maybe he was right to cry, because there's nothing sadder than a sukkah after it's taken apart.

School starts tomorrow. I'm half-scared, half-excited.

scared

excited

Question for the day: Is it wrong to exaggerate
(just a teeny bit) about getting a tetanus shot if it
teaches your little brother a lesson?

MONDAY

This morning, before school, Malka was hogging the
mirror. As usual. She is always staring at herself.
Looking sideways, front, and even over her back. I
can't believe she's only six and cares so much how
she looks. What's going to happen when she turns
ten? Or thirteen? I get scared just thinking about
it. Me, I throw on anything without stains, brush my
hair three times, and I'm done.

"I need to get rid of the bump," she tells me as she
brushes her red hair into a ponytail. Brush, brush.
She takes at least ten minutes.

Maybe that's why she gets the top of her head so
smooth and flat. The top of my own head is always
bumpy when I make a ponytail. But Malka says all
the girls at school have smooth tops. "Every single

one," she insists. "They'll all laugh at me if my head looks bumpy."

my sister
Malka

"Oh, come on, Malka." My sister loves to exaggerate.

Too bad about my doll, Jennie. Her hair still doesn't look normal. I think Deena really ruined her hair this time. But at least Jennie and I are twins with our bumpy-looking heads.

So I go off to school with my bumpy ponytail.
Deena's house is only five minutes away, so I get to
walk to my homeschool by myself. On the way over,
I pass all the girls in their blue skirts and light blue
shirts going off to Bnos Devora. They see me and
usually look away.

Only a little. But I notice it. I don't know why they
do it. Is it because I'm dressed in regular clothes, so
they know I'm not from their school?

Then I notice they all have ponytails, but no bumps
on their heads. Not even the smallest kid has a
bump! Their hair on top is as flat and smooth as an
ironing board. I mean, how do they do that? I guess
they start so young, they get to be real experts
at it. Or they train their hair. That's what happens
when you go to a real school, I guess. So, of course,
me with my bumpy head, I stand out. But still, do
they have to look at me that way? Like I have a
green nose?

Maybe I'm exaggerating, just like Malka.

When I got to school, for the first hour it was so much fun. Everyone started talking about how great their Sukkos was. Then Deena –

Wait. First, let me describe the girls in my school. There's only five, and I already told you about me and Deena, so that leaves only the other three.

There's Miri. She has really skinny wrists and wispy brown hair and reminds me of a dandelion puff. If you sneeze suddenly, she could fly away or disappear. She always has a worried look on her face and says "I'm sorry" a lot. Like if it's raining outside, she'll say "I'm sorry," like it's her fault. Maybe if she wasn't the youngest in the school, she wouldn't apologize so much. I don't know.

She gets a lot of colds and carries around packets of tissues, and the tissues are always falling out of her pockets. I get the feeling that even if she was the oldest one here, instead of the youngest, she'd still be the same.

The next girl is Chedva. She's the oldest - old
enough to be in fifth grade. She looks like a little
angel with dirty-blond curls and freckles. Some
people - they don't really have freckles - they just
have them under their skin and you can barely see
them. Like me. But Chedva's freckles are the real
ones. Everything about her is real.

Whenever she smiles or skips around for no reason,
I get happy, too. She gets excited even about little
things, like going to the library and not even taking
out books for herself, but for her sister. She has a
small oval face and her eyes are like two circles of
diamonds.

Here's a secret: I really, really want to have a play
date with Chedva, but am too shy to ask because
she's a whole year older.

One more thing: she has really bad asthma.
Especially in the springtime.

The last girl is Aviva. Aviva is a brain. That's all I

can say. She's not snobby or anything, but she likes to learn all these facts, like, say, about the clouds, or pollution, or lately, rabbits. So now I know - thanks to Aviva - that rabbits sweat through their feet, they purr like cats, can drink as much water as a dog, are born without fur, and on and on and on.

She can be really fun and interesting, but sometimes she gets on my nerves. All the stuff she talks about, the stuff she reads about, can make me tired. Also, she can be kind of messy and when she eats lunch, sometimes she spills apple juice or tuna fish on my stuff. I hate tuna fish.

But you know what? I have some strange parts, too, right? Aviva doesn't get mad or upset when she can't bring a peanut butter sandwich to school, just because of me. So I won't make a big deal either when she accidentally sprays tuna fish on my pear slices.

So, what was I saying? Oh yeah. Right after

davening, Deena suddenly announced, "After Yom Kippur, I decided to daven the whole Shabbos davening every Shabbos." She added, "Even the things between Ashrei and Yishtabach."

I forgot to tell you something about Deena. She likes to be the most or the greatest or the best at everything. So I guess after Yom Kippur she wanted to be the most religious.

Everyone looked so impressed, especially Chedva. She said, "Wow! I kind of skip those parts."

Then all the girls started telling Morah Zeldy the ways they were going to be better.

"I'm going to say the long Shema every night!"

"I'm going to help my mother every day when I come home."

"I'm going to say Amen to everybody's bracha!"

Soon everyone had said something except for me. I didn't say anything because I couldn't think of what to say.

"Well," Morah Zeldy said, looking my way with her nice blue eyes.

"I'm still thinking," I said. I don't know why, but as soon as I'm expected to say something, suddenly I can't. It's like my tongue turns to mud and the words get stuck. It's like when I'm expected to be friendly, suddenly I freeze up.

Five minutes later, I thought they'd forgotten all about it, but then Deena had to tell Morah Zeldy, "Why isn't Bina saying anything?"

Morah prodded me, "Don't think too hard about it. Whatever comes out ..."

I said, "If my brother messes with my things during breakfast time, I'll count to fifteen before I scream at him."

"What?!" Deena screeched. She started giggling. I don't know why. The others were giggling, too. Even Miri. Even Chedva, who never makes people feel bad.

"Quiet, girls," Morah Zeldy ordered, and so Deena covered her mouth with both hands to stop up her giggle, and then her laughter just sort of snorted out of her, and then all the girls were holding their stomachs, bending over, and laughing. Even Chedva.

Whatever.

I hate it when they giggle at me. I wish I could say something so they'd stop, but I never know what those words should be.

After they finally calmed down, Deena said, "Why only count to fifteen during breakfast?" She turned to Morah Zeldy. "Shouldn't she do it the whole day?"

Morah Zeldy said, "Actually, what Bina said makes a lot of sense. If you try to do too much, you could end up with nothing."

Later Deena threw her arm around me and said,
"Sorry for laughing. It was just the way you said it.
It really is a great idea. Are you mad at me?"

I said no, because it's too boring to stay mad, and
then, because it's Parshas Noach, the teacher had
us all go outside to the ballpark with a super-duper
long measuring tape. Then we measured out how
big the teivah was - three hundred amos by fifty
by thirty. It was kind of cool. Deena and I hopped
backwards down the whole field until finally we fell
onto our backs and couldn't stop laughing.

So in the end it was kind of a nice day.
Guess what? On this Rosh Chodesh, when we go
visit a tzaddekes, we're all going to the home of
the Wedding Gown Lady. She lends out wedding
gowns to lots of brides. A "gemach," it's called. I
can't wait. Maybe they'll let us try on the dresses!

Question of the day: If I start davening the whole
davening on Shabbos, will Deena call me a copycat?

FRIDAY

Today, just as I was walking out the door, I bumped into Shaindy on the sidewalk in front of my house. She looked kind of sad. I asked her what's wrong. Even her boingy blond curls looked sort of limp and sad. She said, "They mixed up all the classes and I don't have any good friends in my class anymore."

"I'm sorry," I said, though inside I thought, So what? There's so many girls in her class to choose from, she can just pick somebody else. She's lucky! The only one my age is Deena. If we get into a fight, then I have no one. "But can't you play with your old friends during recess?"

"Yeah." She kicked a stone on the sidewalk. "I did that at first. But now," she shrugged, "it's not the same. They don't play Chinese Jump Rope anymore. Just Double Jump Rope." She sighed. "I'm not so good at that."

"Oh." I can hardly deal with regular jump rope. Her life sure is complicated.

Suddenly she turned to me. "Hey, want to come to my house tomorrow? For like, uh, a play date?"

Wow! That's the first time Shaindy invited me for a play date on Shabbos!

"Sure!" We set a time. Then she made a right on Walnut Street to go to her school, and I made a left on Walnut Street to go to mine. I passed a bunch of girls from her school, and they gave me that look again. Usually it's the Sideways Look – when they look at you out of the corner of their eyes. Only today it was the Up-and-Down Look. You know what that's like. They started by looking at my Mary Jane shoes (they all were wearing loafers), and then they looked at my socks. I don't know what's wrong with them. All I know is mine don't look like theirs. And then their look slowly climbed all the way to the top of my bumpy head. And that's where their eyes stayed for just a second too long. Grrrr!

One of them, with a cute blond ponytail, made an

open fan out of her hand and talked behind it to
another girl. The other girl laughed.

Uchhh! I hate it when they do that fan thing. I hate
it when girls act like snobs. It makes me boil up
inside like a tomato about to burst. They look at
me like I'm wrong, like I stole something or smell bad,
when all I did is not dress the exact same way as
them and have a bumpy head.

Luckily, I had a play date with Shaindy in my pocket
for Shabbos, and by the time I got to school, I
practically forgot about those snobby girls.

After davening, everyone had to go to their "work
places." That's what it's called in Monty Sorry.
I'm doing a whole project about the thirty-nine
melachos of Shabbos. I'm reading a book about it
that explains everything, and I'm making my own
scrapbook and it's really interesting. I go to Morah
Zeldy when I don't understand the complicated
parts like borer - that's selecting - and tochein -
grinding.

Then, I was in the middle of making my picture of
sewing for my scrapbook – I drew a needle and a
thread and a big fat blue button – when Chedva
came over to see what I was doing. She didn't make
any noise, she just watched me. When I finished,
she said, "That's so cool! How did you draw that
button to make it look so real?"

So I showed her, and then she showed me her
39 melachos scrapbook and we were comparing
melachos – like what she drew for plowing and what
I drew. "You took art lessons?" I asked, and she
said she was going to ask me the same thing! We
were having so much fun and I was thinking, Maybe,
maybe I'll have the guts to ask her for a play date
one day, but always I'm too shy, because she's older
and maybe she'll say no, but then I looked up.

There was Deena standing like a foot away, looking
at us with her arms folded and her cold, cold eyes
looking right through me, like I wasn't there. I never
knew her eyes could look so scary.

"Hey, Deena," I said. She just sniffed a little and turned away.

I sat next to her at lunch, like I always do, but then she got up and sat next to Miri and whispered a joke in her ear. Miri looked pretty happy.

Finally, when Deena was washing her plate - we eat on real dishes and we have to clean up afterward - I said to her, "Why are you mad at me?"

She said in that cold, hard voice, "You know why," and she lifted one shoulder and walked away.

But I didn't know why.

Or maybe I did - a little.

I followed her. "Since when can't I talk to Chedva?"

She bunched her lips together till they came to a point, like the tip of a lemon, and her pale green eyes were blazing at me. "It's the way you did it," she hissed. "Laughing and pretending like I wasn't standing right there." She paused. I saw a lump go up and down her throat. "Like I was a nothing. You were trying to make me feed bad."

"But, but -" I tried to explain that we were just having fun, that I didn't mean to hurt her, but the words wouldn't come out. The scary thing about me is, if somebody says something bad about me,

suddenly I believe them. If a kid says, "You're dumb,"
suddenly I turn into an idiot. If somebody says I
stole or cheated, my first thought is, Hey, did I?

"I'm sorry," I whispered.

She sniffed. "Oh, who cares." She flipped her hand
like she was tossing a tissue into the garbage. Then
she got up and went over to Chedva and started
talking, asking her if she could teach her how to
draw something ... I couldn't hear what. And for the
rest of the day, whenever there was free play, the
two of them were together, planning something.

Ouch.

I don't know why, but just looking at them made
my stomach get all pretzelled up. I wish I could be
like Deena and just go up to Chedva and say, "Hey,
let's play," just because I felt like it. Also, I get real
nervous - because if I don't have Deena as my best
friend, who will I play with? Who will I have? Miri's
not my type, and no matter how hard I try, Aviva

isn't either. If only I'd had the guts to ask Chedva
for a play date.

That's when I realized something. If I like somebody,
I'd better hide it from Deena, because she doesn't
like it when I'm friends with other girls.

Question for the day: If I wear a bathing cap to
sleep, will that get rid of my bump?

SUNDAY

It's a good thing I'd made a play date with Shaindy on
Shabbos, because Deena for sure wasn't coming.
I begged my mother to buy Candy Planet and
gummy bears and barbecue potato chips, because I
wanted to serve normal nosh, and guess what - Ima
bought them!

She says I can eat the gummy bears, but I have
to brush my teeth the FIRST SECOND, right after
Shabbos. She tells me that our dentist is always
saying, "Thanks to Shabbos parties, there will

always be children with cavities, and I'll always make
a good living!"

Shaindy and I played Pick-up Sticks and Tumble and
Guess Who and ten other games, and I was having a
nice time and thinking, Hey, maybe she'll come every
Shabbos and I won't even miss Deena one bit, until
those terrible words plopped out of her mouth: "I'm
bored."

Yikes. Whenever I hear those words, my palms
start getting sweaty. I hate it when girls say

that, because suddenly I feel all this pressure to be exciting and do something, anything so they won't be bored for even a teeny tiny second, and that it's all my fault, and I must have a really boring house or something. Boy, oh boy. When Deena comes over, if it starts to get boring, then we just make it fun. We put on circus shows and talent shows and make up dance steps and songs.

I said fast to Shaindy, "Want to make a circus show?"

She crinkled her nose. "What's that?"

I took out three hula hoops - that's for the three-ring circus - and started explaining how it works, with the lion tamer and the lady who rides the horse, and Shaindy sort of got into it, especially when we took out all my stuffed toys and lined them up to jump through the hoops.

Then we ate tons of nosh. When Shaindy left, she said, "Let's do this again!"

"Sure!" I said.

I felt so happy it almost took away that sting-y
feeling inside me that Deena's still angry at me.
But I can't forget. I'll be eating cereal or brushing
my hair and suddenly I'll remember, and I then my
stomach starts to do the pretzel thing, knotting
up and all, and my heart gets that scared, sad
sting-y feeling. What if she gives me that cold
mean look on Monday?

Later, after Shabbos, I said to my sister Malka who
was jumping rope, "Do you like going to school?"
Thwack, thwack went the rope. She said, "No, I hate
it." Thwack, thwack.

She didn't miss a beat. Well, you know what? I don't
believe her. She just said that because she knows
that's what kids are supposed to say: "School is
awwwful, terrrrible, I haaaate it!" But I see her each
morning with her knapsack and loafers that she
keeps shiny, and her special knee-highs that look like
all the other girls', and she's always excited to go.

And I am excited to go to school, too. But not when my best friend hates me.

Right after Shabbos, I brushed my teeth extra hard so Ima will buy me tons of nosh next time I have Shaindy over. But now my gums kind of hurt from all that tooth brushing.

Question for the day: If I went to Shaindy's school, would I have more friends there?

MONDAY
It's Rosh Chodesh. What a day, what a day, what a day.

On the way over to school, I had a pit in my stomach as big as an egg. I was scared to see Deena, that's why. Especially since the homeschool is in her home and the principal is sort of her mother. But as soon as I walked in, Deena ran up to me and put both hands on my shoulders and said, "We're going to the Wedding Gown Lady!" She started doing some fancy dance steps like at weddings, then she grabbed both my hands and whirled me around.

I couldn't believe it. It was like she was never mad at me! Hurray!

We sat next to each other in the car ride over there, while Aviva and Miri sat next to each other, and poor Miri had to hear all about Aviva's favorite ways to eat tuna fish - tuna fish with mayonnaise, tuna fish with celery and pickles and mustard, tuna fish with cheese, and on and on. Chedva sat near the teacher.

Deena and I played the rock-paper-scissors-shoot game and then sang Miss Lucy until Morah Zeldy asked us to stop. Morah Zeldy was wearing a totally different outfit today that she never wore before. A purplish thing with pale yellow stripes on the cuffs of the sleeves. It's pretty, but I like her regular outfits, the ones that go according to the days of the week. But I guess she wanted to look extra nice because of Rosh Chodesh.

The Wedding Gown Lady had on a short blond shaitel and a real pretty smile. You could just see she would make a kallah who wanted to try on gowns feel comfortable. She showed us all the closets with the hanging dresses. Some with beads, some with lace, some made out of satin, silk, or fluffy stuff called "organza" and "tulle."

"Simple is in," said the Gown lady, "and fussy is out. But there is every kind of gown here that you could want. A gown for everyone." It was like being in a regular kallah store.

The Gown Lady let us try on headpieces. I put one on and felt like I was inside a cloud. Morah Zeldy took pictures of us all singing and dancing in our headpieces.

The Gown Lady is so special. One day, when I grow up, maybe I'll run a gemach for brides, too. Maybe I'll make it a special kind of gemach, say for really short kallahs or really tall ones, or maybe kallahs with really long arms.

Suddenly Morah Zeldy had to leave for a half-hour to pick up lunch for us: whole wheat pizzas!

After she left, the Gown Lady brought out a platter of cookies - not the store-bought kind but the homemade kind. We all looked at each other. The rule is: No nosh in school. Pretzels and popcorn and soy chips, okay. Don't even think about potato chips or cookies in school. But this was out of school, right?

The Gown Lady started talking about gemachs - which just means lending things out for free. She said, "Everybody can start one. You and you and you." She pointed to each of us.

"Everyone try to think of a gemach that you could start," she said.

I wanted to tell her about my idea for a wedding gown gemach for short and tall brides, but I thought, Will she think I'm a copycat, doing almost the same thing as her? And what if everybody laughs at my idea?

While I was thinking this over, my eyes kept staring at those cookies on the platter. Actually, those cookies were looking at me. Eat me, they said. Don't wait for the gemach lady to stop talking. Eat me now before Morah Zeldy returns and says no.

The Gown Lady was looking at Miri. "Can you think of a gemach?"

Miri looked frightened. "Maybe a gemach for - cookies?"

The lady looked puzzled, then she smiled. "That's a cute idea." She turned to me. "Any other ideas?"

The Special Kallah Wedding gemach disappeared out of my head. Instead I said, "How about one for headbands?"

The Gown Lady clapped her hands together. "Brilliant! I love it! What's your name again?"

I gave a modest smile. "Bina Lobell." Maybe I would

start a headband gemach. It would be cool and a
mitzvah, too.

Then Deena threw in, "What about lice, though? If you
share headbands, you could be passing on the lice."

Huh? I thought the gemach lady would say,
Ridiculous! But she nodded her head like Deena
had just said the smartest thing. "How true! And
what's your name?"

Deena said, "Deena Berman."

Meanwhile, Aviva started rattling off all these
gemachs that went through her head: "A sock

gemach, a lamp gemach, a medicine gemach, a dog collar gemach, a toothbrush gemach, a hamster gemach ..."

The Gemach Lady raised her hand, laughing. "Boy, you think fast!"

If she only knew how fast Aviva's mind worked.

I tried so hard to think of another gemach, but this amazing smell from the cookies started prickling my nose. In fact, my nose was itching like crazy. I thought, How could we all insult the Gown Lady by saying no to the cookies she probably baked? Aviva must've been thinking the same thing because she reached for one.

Aviva made a bracha. She chomped really hard, making the crumbs fly. I told you she was messy, right? "Delicious," she said in a muffled voice and reached for another.

There weren't that many cookies on the plate, so

I took one fast before they all disappeared into Aviva's mouth. I made a quick bracha before Morah Zeldy returned, and bit into it. I chewed, I swallowed. What a cookie! Every chew and swallow made my stomach smile. I wanted to write a poem to that cookie, that's how good it was, but of course I said nothing, because even to me that sounds a little crazy. The platter was going around and around and everybody was taking. Suddenly, there were only two left, and I saw Aviva reaching for another - her third! Why should she get three when I only got one? I snatched it before she put her sticky fingers on it and I popped it into my mouth.

Deena shot me a really, really angry look. Maybe I should've broken it in half and shared it. But would she have done the same for me? Maybe, maybe not. Still. I should've shared.

The strange thing is, as I chewed and swallowed, I kept waiting for that happy, glad, wonderful feeling to happen in my stomach. But it didn't happen. No, it didn't. Actually, I started to feel more itchy. And hot. My throat felt like it was getting smaller and smaller, like even spit couldn't go down.

Oh my gosh, oh my gosh, oh my gosh. There was peanut butter inside those cookies. Yes, I could taste it. PEANUT BUTTER!!! I felt a roaring sound in my ears. Peanut butter, oy vey! I jumped to my feet. Little red dots were breaking out all over my arms. I couldn't talk.

The Gown Lady was staring at me. "Is something wrong with the cookies?"

All the girls were just staring at me. I wanted to shout "EpiPen!" but I couldn't. My mouth was on fire; I couldn't talk. I couldn't even remember where I put my knapsack. But if I didn't get that EpiPen soon, I could - die! Why weren't the girls saying something? Why were they just sitting there with their mouths hanging open like that? I wanted to shake them! Then I remembered. They'd never seen me have an attack before. But Deena had seen me once. She was looking at me, frozen, terrified.

I couldn't breathe. I pointed to my throat. "Aaaa," I choked out.

Suddenly Deena shook herself. She pointed. "Get Bina's knapsack over there!" She shouted, "Call 911!" Everyone did just what she said. Somebody gave me the EpiPen. I jabbed it into my leg just like Ima and Abba taught me.

I fell back against the couch where I'd been sitting. Just then Morah Zeldy walked in smiling with a huge whole wheat pizza pie. As scared as I was, I could still smell that pizza. Morah Zeldy took one look at the EpiPen still in my hand and knew exactly what had happened.

"Did Bina already give herself the shot?" Morah Zeldy nearly shouted.

"Yes, yes." The Gown Lady looked scared to death. "It was my peanut butter cookies, oy vey," she mumbled, her hands on her cheeks. Everybody was running around, scared and shouting. I wanted to

say, *Calm down* - I can breathe better now, but
to tell you the truth, it was kind of exciting seeing
everybody running around like that, everyone so
worried about me.

Morah Zeldy held me and walked me over to her
minivan. "She's got to get to the hospital now.
Where's the closest emergency room?"

And so while my whole class was eating pizza, I had
to be in the emergency room with Morah Zeldy,
getting treated. And then have all the adults - the
doctor, Ima, and Abba who came rushing over as
soon as they heard, the nurse - all of them explain
to me for the twentieth time why I should never
eat anything without asking what the ingredients
are. That part wasn't exciting one bit.

Well, most of the time I remember to ask about
the ingredients. But to remember for the rest of
my life?!

Ima called up Deena's home and spoke to Deena,

and thanked her for being the hero and saving the day. I was on the phone and thanked her, too.

"Wow. I guess I really did save your life," said Deena, "which is the biggest mitzvah in the whole world!"

That's true. But a little tiny part of me wanted to ask, So why did it take you so long to tell everyone? Didn't you know how scared I was?

But that's just the yetzer hara talking. Morah Zeldy says that all the time.

Question for the day: Did someone maybe save me a slice of pizza?

TWO WEEKS LATER, THURSDAY

Sorry it took me so long to write in you, Diary. After all that excitement, I just didn't have the strength.

Ima is hovering over me, making sure I'm eating the right things. I wish she wouldn't get so nervous. Just yesterday she told me about a little boy with peanut allergies who held hands with a boy who had eaten a bag of peanut-flavored chips like an hour earlier - a whole hour, Ima kept saying. He must have rubbed his eyes afterwards, and that was enough to make him have an attack.

Ima's eyes get huge when she tells me this story, and I can just see she's trying to figure out how to ask people NEVER to eat anything with peanut butter in it. I imagine Ima going to speak with the Mayor of Cleveland and the President of the United States to make some law and take all the peanuts in the world and dump them into the Atlantic Ocean. I know she never would, but still ...

Anyway, today as I'm getting dressed for school
Malka takes my last pair of socks. "Give them back," I
say. "You've got tons of socks to wear."

Well, she really only has one other pair. I fling her
last pair on her bed and a big, disgusted look comes
over her whole face. "I can't wear that!"

"Why not?"

She holds the toe of one sock like it's a dead mouse.
"It's got pink dots on it."

"So? They look cute," I tell her. They really do. If they
fit me, I'd for sure wear them.

"Nobody wears them," Malky wails. "They'll laugh at me
if I wear them." And because she does look sort of
terrified, I give in and let her wear my blue socks which
are a little small on me and a little big on her.

I borrow my mother's knee-high stockings instead,
then I head off to school. They bag on me a little,

but at least I saved my sister from the sock police putting her in jail.

It's the best part of fall, when all the leaves are dropping left and right and up and down. There's a game I made up ....

But wait - forget that! Lately, I can't stop getting a strange feeling. About Deena.

At school, we'll be playing, laughing, making projects

together, and suddenly she turns away and stops playing with me, and she gets this cool, hard look on her face. Not angry, but not nice either. Sort of like a shark's eyes. I'll look over at her and think, I don't know who my friend is. Who is she? Maybe she's really my enemy.

Yesterday, she suddenly looked up. She said, "Bina, get me a cup of water."

Now that might not sound strange, but it was. Why couldn't she get her own cup of water? Of course, if she had asked me to do a favor because she was in the middle of something, I wouldn't have thought it was so weird. But she just said it like I had no choice. Like she owned me. Get me a cup of water. And I didn't want to. I was going to say, You have legs, don't you? Get yourself a cup! But then I remembered how she'd saved me, and I figured I'd better get her a cup of water without making a big deal about it.

When I gave it to her, she said, "Thanks." But you know how some people say thanks and you feel good, and other girls say thanks like, Okay, now go? That's how she said it. The second way.

And now I'm worried. Because now she probably thinks she can totally be the boss over me. Totally. Worse than before. She'll borrow my erasers and chew the ends and I won't be able to say anything. She'll make me sharpen her pencils, bring her whatever she wants, give her my snacks to eat, borrow my loose-leaf paper and never give any back. That kind of thing.

Or maybe I'm worried about nothing. It was just a cup of water, right?

All I know is I think I better find some other friends. Really really. It's not good to have only one good friend. Because then when you fight, there's no one left and you're really stuck. Yeah, I know I'm always saying that. But I have to get another friend. This just reminded me.

I decided to finally ask Chedva for a play date.

So I went up to her while she was doing a science experiment with seeds. And I'm just watching her, trying to think how to say it, you know, ask for the play date like it's not a big deal, like I just thought of it right now. But Chedva, she's concentrating really hard on her seeds that keep popping out of the soil in the wrong way. One eye is squinched tight and the tip of her tongue is sticking out. And I'm thinking, Should I ask her now or after she gets the seeds in the right way, when Chedva suddenly turns to me and says, "I'm sorry, it makes me nervous when you stand there. I just can't concentrate."

So I left.

So, uh ... whatever.

The thing is, I know she didn't mean to make me feel bad, but I did feel bad, and maybe now it'll take me another two weeks until I get the courage to ask her for a play date.

On the way home, I start playing one of my favorite

games I was going to tell you about - catch the leaves. The leaves start summersaulting down from the high branches, and I try to catch them by making a sandwich with two flat hands, and the leaf is like the salami in the middle. It's so much fun that I don't see the girls from Bnos Devora turning down the street. They see me and they start whispering. Then they start giving me The Look again. I stop shuffling through the leaves. I see them staring at my baggy knee-highs, which were already drooping by then. I just can't take it anymore. I feel so small, so tiny, like I'm going to disappear into a pile of brown leaves and then somebody's shoe is going to step on me.

"It's not nice to stare!" I yell over to them. I can't believe I said that. I feel this pounding in my ears.

They look at me with their eyes popping out. Like I'm a car or chair that just started talking. Their mouths are hanging wide open. And then they all break up laughing and keep on walking.

So I rush home, fast, faster. I feel a hot lump
shooting up my throat. There are so many tears
in my eyes, I can't see where I'm going. Hurry, hurry,
before I break out crying. I just hope Ima's not on
the phone or on the computer, because I need her
to hold me.

I rush up the steps to the porch and almost trip.
I fling open the door. And there's Malka standing
there with mud all over my nice blue socks. She
never cares about my things. I lend them to her and
she treats them like garbage.

I rush over. "You messed up my socks!" I yell. "Take
them off! Now!"

She just looks at me. Levi gets frightened and
sticks his thumb in his mouth.

I scream right into her face, "NOW!"

Malka stares at me like she hasn't heard me. I can't
take it, how no one listens, no one treats me like a

person. I bend down and try to yank off her socks, and Malka tries to kick me away, and that gets me so mad, I pull even harder on her sock, and that's when it happens. She trips and falls and bumps her head on the coffee table.

Malka screams and Ima comes running in from the computer room.

"What did you do?" Ima's eyes blaze. She wraps up Malka, who is still whimpering and crying and rubbing the side of her head, in her arms.

"Why are you always on the computer?" I shout and run up to my room.

So now I'm punished, for good, till forever.

I told you I get angry, didn't I?
I hate everybody. And you know who I hate the most?

Me.

Question for today: When did my little sister get
so smart about hair bumps and not wearing socks
with pink dots, and a million other things?

And when will I get smart?

FRIDAY

This morning, the first thing Malka did when she
woke up (hey, did I tell you we sleep in the same
bedroom?) was she lifted her bangs and showed
me the tiny, hardly-can-see-it little bump on her
forehead. "Look what you did!" she accused me.
I didn't even have a chance to say Modeh Ani. So
this is how I get to wake up?

"I already said I was sorry," I said.

"Not like you meant it!"

I tried to put all the I'm-sorriness I could into my
voice. "I'm really truly sorry, Malka." The funny thing
is, when I said it, I could feel it in my bones. And
maybe Malka could feel it, too. Because she said,

"And I won't mess up your socks anymore."

She's a cute little sister, that Malka, even if all she
cares about is getting rid of the hair bump on
her head. And now she's got a real bump to worry
about. And I am sorry.

Today, during snack time, Morah Zeldy looked inside
everyone's bags to see if they had things that
could cause allergies. Morah Zeldy held up Aviva's
bag of apple soy chips. "Sorry, Aviva, but we can't
allow these."

"But there's no peanuts in it!"

Morah Zeldy pointed to the package. "Look." She
read out loud, "Made in a facility with peanuts. May
contain traces of peanuts and other tree nuts."
I stopped listening. I loved the sound of that word
- "fah-silly-tee" - like the name I'd want to give to
my prettiest doll. But what was this? Why did Aviva
look so angry?

"That's not fair. We always got to eat this before!"
Aviva said.

"Well, we have to be extra careful now," Morah
explained.

Aviva scrunched up her face. "It only says may
contain. May. It's not definite!"

The teacher bit her lip like she couldn't decide if
that counted as chutzpah. "May counts, too,"
Morah Zeldy decided.

Aviva shot me an angry look. But Chedva was very
nice about it. She said, "We all have to be careful.
Look how we can't have carpets or rugs because of
my asthma."

I wanted to throw my arms around her. But when
Morah Zeldy took away her arrowroot biscuits -
the closest thing in the school to a cookie - that
were also made in a peanut "fah-silly-tee," she gave
me a sad look, too. Couldn't help it, I guess. Oh no. I

felt like the snack thief. Because of ME everybody's favorite snacks were getting taken away. I felt my neck and ears and even my nose getting hot and red and even redder.

Morah Zeldy said, "We'll turn it into a good thing. We'll make some of our own snacks or we'll just have to try eating healthier, tastier food."

Now everybody was glaring at me, even Miri, the youngest. Deena had to say, "But peanuts are good for you! They're healthy, too. How come we're not allowed to eat something healthy?"

For a second Morah looked stumped.

Then Chedva said, "Come on. Every person has problems. Some you can see right away on the outside, and some are hidden on the inside. We all have to stick together and help each other."

Morah Zeldy said, "That's exactly right, Chedva. Kol Yisrael areivim zeh b'zeh. It means we're all connected and responsible for each other."

We looked at each other. I know I have a problem
and Chedva has a problem with her asthma. And
Aviva is super-super-smart and Miri is super-shy -
did those count as problems? I dunno. But Deena -

Deena crossed her arms just then. "I don't have a
problem! I'm here only because my mother thinks
Monty Sorry is the best way to teach and it's her
school! It's not fair! Why should I suffer because of
all of you?"

She looked up and saw all of us staring at her kind
of strangely. Even Morah Zeldy was giving her a
funny look. Because, you know, she was sort of
making everybody in the whole room, the whole
school, feel bad.

"Girls," Morah Zeldy clapped her hands, "let's get
back to work."

That's what they call studying in a Monty Sorry

school. Work. She went to the kitchen area to prepare a science experiment that showed how canals operate.

"So," Chedva said after Morah Zeldy left, "are you saying you don't want to be stuck with us?" She was speaking directly to Deena.

For the first time Deena looked a little nervous. We'd never heard Chedva speak that way before. Angry-like. Fire coming from her eyes, like.

"Yeah," Aviva threw in, "is that what you're saying?" She took a step closer, and her fists were tight and hard at her side.

Deena had a help-save-me look on her face. She licked her lips. "I- uh -"

I could feel in my own stomach how scared she was. That's when I stepped up and put my arm around her.

"Deena's just upset because she wants her snack," I said loudly. "You know what? I'll ask my mother to bake us all breakfast cookies tomorrow." Everybody's eyes lit up, because my mother's breakfast cookies are amazing and so healthy, even Morah Zeldy will eat them and allow them in the school.

The strange thing is, you'd think Deena would be happy that I saved her. But she wouldn't talk to me the rest of the day.

I don't understand. I don't understand anything. Hashem, could you please help me understand?

On the way home, I saw Shaindy from far off.
Shaindy! I waited for her to come close so we could
walk the rest of the way home together. I could
tell it was Shaindy because I saw her boingy curls.
She's the only one with hair like that. And also I
recognized her walk. She tilts to one side, kind of.

I waited and waited, squinting, and then, that's
when I saw she was walking with her. Her. You know,
Blond Ponytail, the one who made me feel like ear
wax. I got that pit-in-my-stomach feeling. What
would she say? Would she make fun of me again?
But that's not what I was afraid of. I wondered
what Shaindy would do. Would she say hello to me or
pretend she didn't know me?

I didn't wait around to find out. I picked up my feet
and ran home as fast as I could.

When I got home, Ima asked, "What's wrong?"

"Nothing!" I said. "Nothing, nothing, nothing!"

Question for the day: Why doesn't somebody start a friend gemach? Because that's what I need.

TUESDAY

There's a place in the Shemoneh Esrei where you can ask Hashem for whatever you want. Morah Zeldy showed me the place in the davening. In the Shema Koleinu part - "hear our voice."

Sometimes I ask for candy or a real American Girl doll or a car with no dents or for Levi's cold to get better. Okay, but now I need a friend. Hashem, could You please help me out? You can make earthquakes and thunder and lightning, so how about sending me a really nice friend? Somebody who'll laugh with me, but not at me. Somebody I don't have to be so careful with all the time that I might say the wrong thing. Someone nice and funny and smart, but not too smart. I mean, not boring smart or show-offy smart, either. Would You do that for me, Hashem? Please? I hope it's not too chutzpahdik to ask.

That's what I've been saying in my davening every day this week. But so far nothing's changed.

I wonder what a friend gemach would look like. Let's say I need a friend to come over for a Shabbos play date on a long summer afternoon - the kind that lasts half a day. I could just go to the friend gemach and say, Give me someone who likes to play Apples to Apples. She can be short or tall, fat or thin. I don't care. As long as she's nice.

Or say a girl is having a birthday party and she's worried that not enough girls will show up. She could go to the friend gemach, too, and order a bunch of friends to come.

Hey, you know what? This friend gemach thing could be a great idea, even for grown-ups! Let's say Ima wants to go to a Torah class, but all her friends are busy, so there's no one to go with. Wouldn't it be cool if she could just go to the friend gemach and say, "I need a friend to go with me to this Torah class. An hour and fifteen minutes at the

most." Then the Gemach Lady would look in her files
and choose just the right woman - dresses like
Ima, talks like Ima, looks a lot like Ima - and then my
mother would feel totally comfortable.

Or what if Abba is giving a speech and he's got
a bunch of jokes in it and he's worried that no
one will "get" them. He could go to the friend
gemach and ask for someone with a great laugh.
You know, the kind of laugh that gets everyone
else laughing. Then, when Abba tells his jokes, the

friend from the gemach - who'll be sitting in the audience - can start laughing like crazy, and next thing you know, the whole room will be laughing.

I know it's just a weird idea, but I tell Ima about it and she claps her hands and laughs and just loves it. Then she gives me a worried look. "Is everything okay at school?" she asks.

I guess she's worried things must be pretty bad if I'm talking about borrowing friends.

I look down and shake my head. I say, "Uh-uh."

She strokes my hair. "It must be hard having only five girls in your class."

"In my whole school!" I add.

She waits for me to talk some more, but I don't say a word because I don't want to choke up or anything. "Hey, Bina," she says. "I have a stamp from Belgium for your collection," and she gives it to me.

I try to look excited as I take it (it is pretty), but
what good is a stamp? It can't laugh at your jokes
or anything.

Later that night I hear her talking to Deena's
mother. They're whispering, planning something,
I don't know what. I catch little words here and
there, "... got to do something ..." "... social skills are
so important, too ..."

They're always talking, trying to find ways to
make the school better. But there's a difference.
For Ima, the school is important. But for Deena's
mother, it's even more. It's her dream. She thinks
every Jewish school in the world should be Monty
Sorry, really creative and small and bringing out the
best in each girl.

The next day, I try to make a play date with
Chedva, but it's just too hard with Deena always
around giving me those weird looks, making me so
nervous.

At home, Ima says, "Why don't you call her up and tell her about that new game you just got for Chanukah, and ask if she wants to come over and play it."

Yeah! I just got Perpetual Commotion. It's so much fun.

But then, "It's dorky to call on the phone," I say. "It's weird. Like I'm making too much out of it."

So she coaches me on how to ask Chedva, coaches me on what to say so I sound normal and like it's not a big deal for me. We practice. First I'm Chedva and Ima is me. And then I'm me and she's Chedva. I practice all my lines even though it feels really weird.

Finally, I dial.

"Uh, Chedva?" My throat feels sort of dry, like Styrofoam.

"Who is this?" Chedva asks in a suspicious voice.

"Just me," I mumble. "Bina." Now my throat feels hot and stuffy.

"Hi, Bina," she says, friendly-like.

"Do you know how to play Perpetual Commotion?" I blurt out really fast.

"Uh huh," she says. "Sure."

"Well, I just got it for Chanukah, and I can't figure out the rules and stuff. Want to come over on Shabbos and show me?"

"Oh, but it's really easy," Chedva says. "All you have to do -" She stops suddenly. "You know what? Sure, I'd love to come. What time?"

My heart's pounding when I get off the phone. I did it! Hurray! I run to the mirror and look at myself. I'm grinning so hard, I look like a chipmunk or something. I skip around the kitchen and Malka and Levi skip with me, even though they have no idea why.

It's time to go to sleep, but I'm too excited. What will we play after Perpetual Commotion? Maybe Apples to Apples? Or Connect Four? What if she doesn't like those games? Okay, then we'll play Chinese Jump Rope. But for that we need an extra person. I guess it'll be okay for Malka to join, but just for a little bit, because I want Chedva all to myself. I'd better get to sleep. I'll say Shema in just a second. Thank you, Hashem, thank you, Hashem, thank you, Hashem!

P.S. I asked Ima how to spell Monty Sorry, and here's the right way: Montessori. I think. But you know what? I like my way better.

Question for the day: If it was that easy to make a play date with Chedva, why didn't I do it a year ago?

JUST AFTER SHABBOS
I can't believe it. Everything got ruined. RUINED. And it's all because of that phone call Ima made.

Why did she have to talk about my problems to
Deena's mother? Why did Deena's mother have
to plan a whole big Shabbos get-together on the
very same Shabbos I had my first play date with
Chedva? So the whole school had to come to this
get-together at Deena's house. All five of us.
Something to do with socializing. All the mothers
decided we should be having more play dates and
fun times together.

More time together? More?

Yikes.

I told Ima I wasn't gonna go, but she explained how
Deena's mother worked so hard to make it special
and baked these healthy cakes and planned a million
exciting games.

"Come on, honey. Just go to the party," she
coaxed me. "And then get together with Chedva
afterward."

I thought it over. You know what? I could do both, just like Ima said.

When I got to the Bermans' house on Shabbos afternoon, I saw all these balloons and party streamers hanging from the ceiling. I don't know why, but it didn't give me a good feeling. First off, it wasn't anyone's birthday. And it was just like Ima said. Deena's mother had worked hard to make it a nice party. But that was just the problem. Mrs. Berman worked too hard. Way too hard.

Deena's mother clapped her hands. "Come along, girls!" She took out a whole complicated game of Bingo based on the thirty-nine melachos. She'd made it up herself. It must've taken her hours.

I was about to sit next to Chedva, but Deena just sort of slipped in and took my spot. Then she smiled at me with that innocent look on her face.

So what? I told myself. I have a play date afterward. With Chedva.

The Bingo game was fun. If only Mrs. Berman had stopped there and then sent us home.

Instead she called us to the kitchen. There were apples and pears and kiwis and watermelon spread out on the kitchen table with cutting knives. Mrs. Berman taught us how to cut up fruit to make it look neat and pretty.

Deena said, "Your kiwi looks like a sick spider."

I said, "Yours looks like frizzy hair."

Just then Mrs. Berman passed by and said, "Now girls, let's speak nicely," but she was looking at ME, like I was the one who started it. No fair. Then we ate the fruit.

Okay, so now could we go? We'd already been there for ninety whole minutes. But then Mrs. Berman came out with five decks of cards. "Guess what, girls?" She gave this dramatic pause. "We're playing five-deck Memory!"

Oy! Now I'd be stuck there forever! But what could I do? She handed out five decks of cards and we all dropped to the floor and began spreading out the cards.

Actually, I like Memory, because my memory is pretty good, but my head was dizzy and my eyes were swimming from turning over all those cards and trying to find matches. And Mrs. Berman kept saying in this excited voice, "Girls, isn't this fun?" Actually, maybe it would've been fun if I hadn't wanted to go to the play date already.

Finally, it ended. I didn't even care who won. I stood up to get my coat, but then Mrs. Berman came out with another game, who even remembers what. By now, I was going crazy, just crazy. We'd been there two-and-a-half hours.

I kept looking at Chedva as if to say, Let's get out of here! And she'd look back and spread out her hands like she was saying, But how? Finally, it started to get a little dark outside and now Mrs.

Berman announced in this big, excited voice, "Girls, time for Shalosh Seudos."

Argggh!

At least the agave cake was great. Too bad Deena was the one cutting the slices. Of course she gave herself and Chedva the biggest slices. Me, she gave the smallest. I don't really care. But how come Mrs. Berman didn't notice - not even once - when Deena wasn't acting nice? I mean, the school is in her own

house. How come she doesn't open her eyes and ears and pay attention?

But maybe it's not her fault. Deena knows how to save her really mean behavior for when no one's around. That's her real talent. Knowing just how much to get away with in front of adults.

But here was the really bad, horrible, no-fair part. After Shabbos, Deena said to Chedva, "You want to go swimming at the Y? They're having Motza'ei Shabbos Madness!"

I felt like someone just threw a pie smack in my face.

I almost rushed over and screamed, "You can't do that! Chedva was supposed to have a play date with me. ME! Got that?" But it was like she'd punched all the words out of me.

If only Chedva would've said that she already had a play date. Instead she said, "Great! I love swimming!"

A minute later she looked at me, then covered her mouth, like Uh-oh. What did I just say?

Whatever.

Later, Chedva came up to me. "Sorry it didn't work out," she whispered. I wonder why she whispered. Is she getting scared of Deena, too?

So now at this very second, Chedva and Deena are splashing around in the pool at the Y and I'm home alone. And it's all Ima's fault.

Ima said, "So just call Chedva again. Make another play date."

What's the point? Deena will just take her away. She always does. I'll never be as strong as Deena. She always wins.

I don't even have the strength to ask any more questions like I usually do at the end of the day in my diary. I'm too tired.

A whole month has passed. It's February now.

WEDNESDAY
Okay, I know I should've written something.
Anything. But what's the point? There's nothing to
say. Every day in school is boring. Okay, maybe not
totally boring. We're doing something really cool to
learn about all the states, something called "State-
in-a-box." We also visited another tzaddekes who
designs cool pushkah boxes. I really like her. She
taught us how to make a bracelet and a necklace
out of rocks. Morah Zeldy has been teaching us the
blessings of Yaakov, and we made up a whole song
and dance, and performed it for our mothers and
grandmothers. That was great.

But it's so boring how every day Chedva and Deena
come in wearing a dumb matching bow in their
hair. Or matching socks. Or they bring the same
sandwich. I can't stand how they giggle about

such dopey things. They're best friends now. BEST FRIENDS!

I can't stand watching them.

Every day they sit next to each other during lunch and talk, talk, talk. Or they play a game where they take the same number of bites out of their sandwiches so they finish at the same exact time. They think they're so so funny. But they're not. They're sooo not funny.

What I hate most is when they whisper to each other. Whisper, whisper. You don't know if they're talking about you, or just talking so you don't hear, or just whispering to get you curious. To me a whisper is worse than a kid hitting you.

And who do I sit next to? Miri and Aviva. Miri's just too young and too scared and shy to be a real friend, and Aviva talks so much, she just hurts my brain. These days she's into spiders. She's got a whole list of spider facts. How there are

40,000 different kinds. And how they're really called "arachnids," or something like that, and how a left-behind spider web is called a cob web, and how spiders live everywhere in the world except Antartica - important things like that. She keeps going on and on. There's no stopping her. Help! And I don't even like spiders.

The truth is, I didn't write in here for so long because whenever I stare at the pages, my eyes start to sting. Like I could cry or something.

I don't even look forward to going out to see the next tzaddekes of the month.

I just don't understand Chedva. Can't she see that I'm much more fun to be with than Deena? How come she doesn't realize that Deena stole her from me? I mean, we had a play date all set up, and then she just goes ahead and forgets all about me? I don't understand anything. Well, maybe I'm not so much fun to play with, after all. Maybe I'm really boring and I don't even know it.

Ima just gives me these sorrowful looks. She keeps saying, "What can we do to put the sparkle back in your eye?"

I shrug. I just mutter, "Send me to a normal school, where there's lots of girls to choose from."

Then I start to think what it would be like to be just regular, like everyone else, just a normal girl, like ... like who? Well, like Shaindy.

Abba walks by just then and asks what me I'm thinking about. So I tell him how I wish I could trade places with Shaindy and how then I wouldn't have any problems at all.

Abba shakes his head, laughing a little. "Binah, everyone has problems. Even Shaindy. Otherwise she wouldn't be a human being."

"Well, how come I can't see any?"

"Just because you can't see them doesn't mean they aren't there," he points out. "But tell me, Bina, would you really want to switch places with Shaindy?"

I stare out the window. At first it seems like a great idea. I'd LOVE to have her boingy curls and go to a normal school and have no allergies, but then I think - I'd be Shaindy and not me, and the jokes I make and the way I think and the funny things that I notice about people - it wouldn't be part of this world. Instead of me there'd be - I don't know - air. My brain itches just thinking about it.

I shake my head. "I don't want to be Shaindy," I say.
"I want to be me, just without allergies."

Then I take my book and read and look out the
window at the others who all seem to have
someone to play with and seem like they don't have
any problems at all.

After a little while, I can hear Abba and Ima talking
in the other room, but I can't hear what they're
saying. Their voices go low and high and then low
again. I know they're talking about me. It kind of
makes me feel good. Because they're discussing me,
you know what I mean? Like I'm the most important
thing in their lives.

But now their voices are getting sharper. Faster.
Louder. Oh, no - a fight. Now I feel bad.

Later, I come down for some water and I hear Abba
and Ima talking some more.

Ima says, "Impossible! The school won't -" I miss a

few words, then Abba says, "You have to at least try." Then quiet voices, and again Ima's voice rises, "What if Bina has another -" Abba interrupts, "You can't protect her forever!" And Ima says, "Why not?"

I'm so curious what they're saying, but I know it's wrong to listen so I just drink my water (very slowly) and go back to my room.

Okay, that's it for today. At least I wrote in my diary. I know I should ask a question. Any question. Abba says, as long as you ask questions, it means you want to hear an answer. It means you haven't given up hope, although I'm not sure what that means. Forget it. Anyway, I just can't think of any questions.

Wait. Question for the day: Could somebody please invent a tube of sparkly stuff so I can get the sparkle put back into my eyes?

A WEEK LATER, THURSDAY

Yay! Hurray! Oh my goodness. Everything changed.
EVERYTHING CHANGED! CHANGED!!

I'm going to Bnos Devora next year; I'm going to
school with my sister. I'll wear the Bnos Devora
jacket and skirt and I'll get the really expensive
knapsack that all the girls use so I can fit in, and I'm
already practicing every day how to get the head
bump to go down and be flat and smooth. I'll have
twenty girls to choose from to be friends with or
maybe even twenty-five. I won't have to see Chedva
and Deena every day, talking and smiling and not
including me.

Well, that's not fair. Sometimes Chedva tries to
include me, but she stops as soon as Deena comes
into the room. She'll look over her shoulder and
then she'll say something or ask a question in her
friendly way, but as soon as Deena comes back in -
whoosh! - forget it, it's like I don't exist anymore.

You know what? Now I feel sorry for Chedva. I think

Deena has become the boss of her, too. Which is kind of strange because Chedva is a year older.

But I don't even have to think about them. I'm leaving!

Here's what happened. One day, Ima knocked on the Bnos Devora principal's door and started talking and talking and explaining why she had to take me in – that if the public schools were willing to turn their whole schools upside down and make them nut-free, then why couldn't Bnos Devora do it? It would be the biggest chesed. The principal listened but wasn't convinced yet.. "It's a big change for just one girl ...."

Ima said, "It's not just one girl. If your school became nut-free, I know now of many other kids who would be able to attend, instead of having to go to less religious schools, or schools that are far away. Do you know how painful that is, for your child to not have any friends because she has to go to a different kind of school?"

I wasn't there listening, but this was how Ima told
me it went. She even acted it out, showing her
face, then the principal's face, then making it all
exciting and dramatic with her arms clasped, trying
to convince the principal.

Ima went on, "It wouldn't be for just one girl, but at
least ten. Believe me. Think what a big mitzvah you'd
be doing." She throws out her arms to show how
big a mitzvah it is.

Well, Ima knows how to talk. She sure does. The principal said, "You convinced me, Mrs. Lobell. I'll do it."

Ima should get a medal for best mother in the world. Abba says she should've been a lawyer, but Ima hears lawyers talking all day long in her court job and says, "No thanks."

Then she said to me, "Keep this quiet for another week until all the details are settled."

Today I didn't even care that Chedva and Deena were making some cool project out of paper mache and they couldn't bother talking to anybody else. I didn't care that Aviva went on and on about all the different kinds of raisins there are in the world. She actually came to school with seven different boxes, blindfolded me, and made me try them all. They really taste different, you know? But it wasn't exactly my idea of fun.

I didn't care about any of that. Because now I have an escape.

Who knows: Maybe Shaindy will become a real
friend, instead of an I'll-play-with-you-if-there's-
no-one-else-around friend. Or maybe I don't really
care if she becomes my friend or not, because
in a class of twenty-five girls, there's got to be
somebody I'll like. Right? Right! And somebody who'll
like me back.

Abba is always saying, "Salvation comes in the blink
of an eye." Which means, things can be really really
bad, so bad you want to give up, but then Hashem
can turn things around just like that, in the time it
takes to sneeze, or wink, or snap your fingers. Just
like that.

Question for the day: Does Hashem make all
mothers extra brave so that they can stick up for
their kids?

MONDAY
Today I walked into school, saw Miri sitting all by
herself looking so lonely and sad, and I asked,
"What's wrong?"

Usually she just looks down or says, "Nothing," but this time she told me a whole story about a little kitten that had a jar of mayonnaise stuck on its head and couldn't get it off, and how the cat was starving to death and she wanted to save it.

My mouth dropped open. I'd never heard Miri say so many words at one time. And then, what a story about that cat!

I said, "We have to save it."

Miri said, "How? Whenever I get near it, it runs away."

"Poor thing's too scared," I told her. "We have to earn her trust." I can't help talking about a cat like it's a girl. Cats are always cleaning themselves. They're so girly.

So we started talking about what we could do to make her feel safer, and it was so interesting that for a few minutes I forgot I was talking to

Miri, who usually has nothing to say, or if she
does, is too scared to say it. We made plans to
go to Miri's house after school and see what we
could do.

Meanwhile, Deena and Chedva were looking at us
from the corners of their eyes, trying to listen, you
know? But pretending like they weren't. I don't even
care.

When Deena got up to go to the bathroom, Chedva
said, "What's that story I heard about a kitten?"

So we told her, and she got excited and said she
wanted to help, and could she come, too?

Usually I would've been so excited to get together
with her after school, I would've danced around the
room. But now I just shrugged. "Why not?"

Then Deena came back and Chedva sat with her like
she was glued to her side. I think it's kind of scary
or strange when girls get like, I have to sit next

to my friend, like they can't even sneeze without asking permission from their best friend. I hope I never get like that.

I asked Deena's mother to call my mother and ask if I could go to Miri's after school. She said yes.

Meanwhile, Chedva changed her mind about coming. I guess Deena said no or something like that. Poor Chedva.

The kitten likes to hang out under Miri's porch, so I had an idea. If we got a box and put a cozy blanket in there, maybe a pillow, the cat would have some warm place to go on a winter day. So we borrowed an old, but soft blanket that used to belong to Miri and put it in a box, and we waited. After about fifteen minutes, we saw the kitten coming. It was the saddest - and strangest - thing I'd ever seen: this huge glass jar like a space helmet over the kitten's head. Like an astronaut! It was so heavy, the poor kitten could barely walk or hardly see, I bet.

"How long can the poor thing go without eating or drinking?" I mumbled. "Look how skinny it is!"

Miri said, "Maybe if it gets so skinny, the jar will slip right off!"

I looked at her. "Wow, that's really smart, Miri!"

She blushed. Then she quietly added, "But who knows, by that time, the kitten might already be dead."

Also true.

I said, "Let's just move six inches closer, wait a few minutes, and then go another few inches closer."

So that's what we did. Each time we got closer, the kitten would stiffen, raise its head, then drop it down on the blanket. But you could tell it was thinking, trying to decide what to do. Even its tail seemed tense and alert.

By now we were so close, I could touch the box with my shoe. "Okay," I whispered. "Let's go another six inches closer."

Carefully, carefully, we inched closer. The cat's tail starting flicking anxiously. Then it paused. If I reached out, I could yank that jar off, I know I could. I leaned, I leaned, and then -

"Miri, girls, where are you?" Miri's mother called out.

In half a second, the kitten leapt out of the box and scampered out from under the porch.

What a shame! We were so close. So close and yet so far, like Abba sometimes says.

I'm so scared for that poor kitten. Starving to death like that.

Question for the day: Is it okay to say Tehillim for a kitten?

TUESDAY

As soon as I walked into school, Deena sort of made her hand into a fan and began talking to Chedva behind it - you know, whispering. Whisper whisper. Making that sound like a mosquito buzzing, just driving me crazy. But then I thought - Deena wants to get me mad - and I decided, I won't do it, I just won't. I don't have to come back next year; I'm not trapped in this school. That makes me feel - I don't know - like, calm inside. Like I don't have to get so mad.

So Miri and I were talking about the kitten, and then Aviva joined in. "What were you going to do if you caught the cat?" Aviva asked.

"Just yank off the jar, I guess."

"Well, that doesn't make any sense," Aviva said. "It's probably stuck for a good reason."

"Maybe use butter or oil to help slip it off," Miri said.

"Or we could get a hammer and gently break the jar," I said.

"But then glass could fall into its eyes," Aviva pointed out. "Also, what if it's a feral cat?"

"What's a feral cat?" Miri asked, her eyes getting big.

"A dangerous wild kind that scratches, that could hurt you."

"Oh, it doesn't look dangerous," I said, but Aviva said you never can tell.

I couldn't believe all the things Aviva knew about

cats. "So what would you do?" I asked her.

She got a thoughtful look on her face. "I'd just
pick up the box with the cat in it and bring it to
a veterinarian. Only an animal doctor can handle
something like this."

A vet! Of course! Then -

"Forget it," I said. "I know a girl whose cat needed a
stomach operation and it cost $2,000. There's no
way my parents would pay that kind of money."

"Not mine either," Miri said.

We looked at each other, both of us feeling so
sorry for that poor kitten.

"I know!" Chedva said.

We all looked up and turned. Chedva was crocheting
a potholder at another table. Had she been
listening the whole time? "Why not call the Society

for the Protection of Animals?" she said.

"You mean the American Society for the Prevention
of Cruelty to Animals," Aviva corrected her.

"Good idea!" I said.

So you know what? We told Morah Zeldy about
the kitten's problem and she turned it into a whole
class project. She taught us about tza'ar ba'alei
chaim, not being cruel to animals, and we looked
up the Society's number in the phone book, and I
actually called up the place and spoke to one of the
stop-the-cruelty-to-animals guys.

He said he'd come to Miri's porch, so we all got to
leave school and go to Miri's and watch everything.
It was so exciting. First, we all sat and waited and
waited for the cat to show up. Finally, I saw this jar
coming our way, and it was the kitten. Boy, did she
look weak, and so so skinny. I wanted to cry.

The animal guy just stared at the cat, his mouth

hanging open. "I never saw that before!" he said, scratching his jaw. "Looks like it's from outer space."

Somehow he got that cat to trust him pretty fast - maybe it was the tuna fish he had in his hand? Then he scooped the cat up and put it in a big cage.

"Cats sure are curious," the man chuckled. He looked at us just then, then back at Morah Zeldy. "These girls can't all be your daughters, can they?"

Morah Zeldy laughed. "No, we're just a school," she said, then added, "Though sometimes it does feel like a family."

As he got into his van, I asked, "So do you think the cat will be okay?"

He scratched his jaw again. "I think so. You all did the right thing by calling me." He said, "You're all Jewish girls, right? Religious and all that? I can tell, by the way -" He made some kind of wiggly motion, pointing toward our long skirts. We nodded, and he said, "Well, you girls just pray hard for this little cat, all right?"

As he drove off, we all waved good-bye, even Deena.

"Girls," Morah Zeldy said afterward, "you all made me so proud of you."

"Why?" asked Aviva.

"Well, because you cared about the poor cat, and you didn't give up, and you called up the right people, and you behaved so well."

We all nodded. Miri and I looked at each other. We felt so good knowing we'd saved that poor cat.

"Maybe," Miri said in her quiet voice, "we did a kiddush Hashem."

Morah Zeldy said, smiling, "Could be."

It sure was a fun day. A fun two days, actually. But then Deena had to go ahead and almost ruin it. "You made such a kiddush Hashem," she said later to Miri in this awful, making-fun voice, when Morah Zeldy was out of the room. "That's because you're both soooo special."

Miri looked like she was about to cry, but I just said to her, "Ignore her, Miri. Pretend she's just bad weather."

Miri looked at me. "Bad weather," she repeated. She wiped her eyes, stood up a little straighter, and smiled.

Now if only I could follow my own advice.

Question for the day: If Deena was really bad weather, would she be a boiling hot desert, or a hurricane, or a horrible snowstorm?

MONDAY

Miri and I started collecting headbands to start a
headband gemach - we clean them really well so no
one can say they have lice or anything. Sometimes
Aviva joins in, sometimes she doesn't. We just make
sure she doesn't feel left out. I never thought Miri
could be so fun. But she actually is. Even if she's
younger.

Of course, Deena started doing her whisper-
whisper thing behind her hand. "She's just a bad
summer storm," I told myself. Here for now, and
then gone. But my bad-weather trick wasn't
working so well today. You know why?

I started thinking. If Deena is whispering mean
things about me, how come Chedva listens?
How come she smiles and nods her head like she
agrees? She knows she's not supposed to listen
to lashon hara. Some girls, you just know they're
mean, and that's who they are. And some girls are
in-between, mostly nice, but can be mean when
it gets them more friends. But then there's the

third kind - that's who I thought Chedva was - who won't be mean, ever. Because they know it's wrong. Because, like Morah Zeldy would say, it hurts your neshamah.

But on and on it went. Whisper whisper. Giggle, smile, snicker. Grrrr! How long could I ignore this bad weather?

Finally, it was Deena's turn to chop some vegetables in the kitchen for this soup we were having, and I went up to Chedva who was sitting by herself now and experimenting with making different colors using eye droppers.

"How come you listen to lashon hara about me?" The words just fell out of my mouth.

Chedva looked at me, her eyes all innocent. "What are you talking about?" She put down her eye dropper carefully. "Who's saying lashon hara?"

"Come on," I said bitterly. "I know you and Deena

are always whispering about me."

Chedva folded her arms. "We're not talking about you," she said at last. "I mean it."

I couldn't believe it. "But you were," I insisted. I knew what I saw, the way they kept looking at me. I started feeling that mad feeling in the tips of my toes, climbing up my body, about to come screaming out of my mouth. "What happened, Chedva? When did you become a liar?"

"I'm not a liar," she said, but nervous-like. "We weren't talking about you – or anyone." She squeezed the eyedropper and a squirt of paint went into a white dish.

I put my face close to hers. "So what were you saying?"

Chedva shoved out the word slowly: "Watermelon."

Huh? "Watermelon? You expect me to believe that?"

"Yeah, it's like a game. It just sounds like we're talking and saying things." She demonstrated: "Watermelon, watermelon, watermelon." It did sound like a lot of words getting spoken.

"But why -" I broke off, confused. It made no sense. Why make a sound like people are talking that really isn't talking?

Then I understood. I understood it all. Deena and Chedva wanted me to think they were whispering about me, to get me all mad. But of course Chedva would never say or listen to lashon hara, so she and Deena worked out a compromise. They'd say "watermelon" and whisper behind their hands, and then I'd get all angry. Deena would be happy I was getting angry and Chedva could feel okay about herself because she wasn't really saying or listening to lashon hara. If I thought they were - well, that was _my_ problem. And if it was mean to do this, it sure didn't seem to bother her.

I looked down at Chedva. Her face had turned

watermelon red. She knew that I knew. "When did you turn into such a sneaky not-nice person?" I asked her. Her eyes nearly popped out of her head. I didn't even wait for an answer and walked away.

So who did I bump into on the way back to my work table? Deena, of course. "Ouch!" she yelled. "Watch where you're going!"

"You watch where you're going!" I shouted back.

Deena was so surprised I yelled back that she stood there, stunned. Then she stuck her finger a quarter of an inch away from my nose. "You're not our boss. You can't tell us what to say!" she yelled. "Yeah, I heard everything," she smirked. She kept poking her finger real close to my face. "We can say 'watermelon' as much as we want." Her face screwed up. "You just can't stand that you don't have any friends!"

Mrs. Berman and Morah Zeldy came running into the room, just as I shouted back, "Well, so what? Next year I won't have to be in this stupid school anymore!"

The whole room went quiet.

Deena blinked. Miri's lip quivered like she was going
to cry. Morah Zeldy said, "You're leaving, Bina?" Her
face had gone kind of pale.

Mrs. Berman put her hand on Deena's shoulder.
"What about your allergy?" she said in a quiet voice.

"I-uh ..." I had a feeling I was in big trouble. Why
hadn't I kept my big mouth shut? "My mother
worked it out with the school."

Mrs. Berman shook her head. "Surely, my ears can't
be hearing right. How could you be leaving?" Her
voice got higher and higher. "Surely, your mother
would've told me. We're such good friends."

How I wished I hadn't said a word.
Hadn't Ima told me to keep it a secret a little
longer? "Well, it's not final," I said.

Mrs. Berman kept shaking her head. "But - how could your mother do that to me?" she said, twisting her hands together. "How can I run a school with just four girls?"

I started getting really nervous. I wanted to say, "I was joking!" But I wasn't, and it's not a joke.

Deena sneered, "We're not going to have a school anymore! And it's all because of youuu!" She dragged out that last word so that it went on for, like, six seconds.

Everybody came closer and closer. They surrounded me. My head was aching. I almost threw up.

So now guess what? My whole class is mad at me - Miri and Aviva, too - because I'm leaving them, and I bet you even Morah Zeldy is mad at me, too!

Question for the day: How did "watermelon" get to be the word that sounds like lots of people talking? What about "canteloupe" or "gefilte fish"? Or maybe - oh, forget it ....

TUESDAY
WHAT A MESS, WHAT A MESS, WHAT A MESS!

Today I didn't go to school. I'm not going to a place where everyone hates me.

Ima didn't make me go, either. But I don't know how long that's going to last.

There wasn't much to do. Malka was at school; of course Levi was at his playgroup. Abba was at work.

Ima rearranged her court job so that she could
do work at home and stay with me, but she wasn't
happy about it because it means she makes less
money. I played Connect Four against myself. But it
was no fun because I always knew what move I was
going to make. You can't fool yourself.

So I was in the middle of reading a Kidspeak book
when the doorbell rang. I peeked out the window.
Maybe it was my class coming to get me with one
of those Get Well cards they send you when you're
sick, and the whole class signs it and begs you to
come back soon. That's what I was sort of hoping.
Instead, it was Mrs. Berman. Deena's mother.

Ima sent me upstairs while the two of them sat
down to talk. I missed a lot of it, but then I got
thirsty and came down for a drink.

So here's what I heard on the way to the kitchen.

Deena's mother: "... I can't run a school that way ..."

Ima: "... I understand, but can't you see I have to do what's best for my daughter?"

(I opened the cupboard very slowly, so there'd be no squeaks.)

Deena's mother: "... our girls get individual attention, they're growing in their middos, their test scores put them at the very top ..."

Ima: "True, true, you did an amazing job ..."

Deena's mother: "Did. Did! You're speaking in the past tense. Like there's no changing your mind."

(Now I took out a cup, careful, so as not to make noise.)

Ima: "... but Bina's so unhappy ... she has no friends, she feels ..."

Deena's mother: "These girls, one minute they're enemies, the next minute best friends forever!

How can you make a decision based on a child's mood? ..."

(I very quietly turned on the faucet.)

Suddenly Ima stuck her head into the kitchen and saw me. She pointed upward toward my bedroom. When I saw that look on her face I went. Fast.

But ten minutes later, I was thirsty again. Really. No, really. I crept downstairs.

Deena's mother: "... the school's my dream. Do your realize if Bina goes, then all the girls will leave?"

(I took a step into the kitchen.)

Ima: "... I thought the dream was to do what's best for our girls. We feel it's best for our daughter to be in a regular school, especially now since the school can accommodate her peanut allergy."

Deena's mother: "But what about my school?

Because if there's only four girls, I don't have a
school and you know it ..."

(Another slooow step.)

Ima: (long pause) "I'm so sorry. We all began this with
such high hopes."

Deena's mother: "Please, Shoshy," (that's my
mother's name) "let's try to work this out. I know if
we try hard, we could."

I took another baby step. Finally Ima said, "If only it
were possible."

"Why isn't it? Deena will help out. The girls listen
to her, you know. Before you know it, they'll all be
getting along just like they used to."

Hah! I thought. Right.

Now it got real quiet.

"I don't know if you're aware," Ima finally said in a careful voice, " but it seems - and I could be wrong - that Deena has turned the class against Bina."

Shocked silence. Then ...

"How could you believe that lashon hara?" Deena's mother sputtered. "Why, I can't believe what I'm hearing! I don't believe a word!"

"I'm not saying I believe it 100% either," Ima answered back, "but all I know is, Bina can't bear the thought of going to school. And I have to pay attention."

ATCHOOO!

Oy, why did I have to sneeze at the best part? Quick, before Ima could catch me, I scampered up the stairs.

Oh, my goodness. I kept thinking about how Mrs. Berman must be angry at me. But now I see that she and Ima are mad at each other. And they used to be best friends!

I went into my bedroom and climbed under the covers. This whole mess is my fault! How could I destroy Mrs. Berman's school? Because that's what I'm doing.

I wish, I wish – I don't even know what to wish. I wish things were simple again. I wish everybody got along. I wish I didn't have a peanut allergy. Really, I just wish I could hide under the covers and never come out.

Question for the day: Is there a difference
between wishing for something and davening for
something?

WEDNESDAY

I was lying in bed while Malka got dressed. As usual,
she spent fifteen minutes getting rid of the bump
on her head. She wanted to borrow my socks,
my last good pair, but I grabbed them back. Just
in case. Malka said, "Not fair. You're not going to
school and you're not even sick!"

So Ima called out from another room, "Oh yes she is
going!"

I yelled, "They hate me, Ima! My whole class!"

"No, they don't, Bina. Don't get carried away."

Well, glad I held onto my socks. Though I wasn't glad
about going to school.

I learned about similes last week. That's when

things are "like" something else. While I was walking
to school, I felt like I was walking through ten feet
of smelly mud. Seeing Deena and Chedva and Aviva
and Miri playing together so nicely without me
was like swallowing a bucket of snake poison. I felt
so different from everybody, so apart, like, like, a
pickle on a plate of marshmallows. Like I just didn't
belong. Okay, I think I'm sick of similes for now.

I thought Mrs. Berman wasn't going to smile at
me like she usually does whenever I come to her
house for school. But she did. Her eyes didn't shine,
though, like they usually do. I could see she seemed
hurt and upset still, but she wasn't saying anything.

I hung up my knapsack and got ready for davening.

Aviva looked to make sure Deena wasn't around.
"Guess what? They got the jar off the kitten."

Miri peeped at me. "And my mother said we can
adopt her," she said real fast before Deena got
back.

"Great," I said. But since when was even Aviva scared of Deena? I'm gone for one day and look what happens. Everybody changes. Everybody.

At first, school wasn't that bad. At least I wasn't moping around at home, waiting for the big excitement of the day - Levi to get back from playgroup.

Today Morah Zeldy made a whole tea party, but the trick was to say everything in Hebrew. Ani emzog lach kos tay - "I'll pour you a cup of tea," I said to Miri.

"At rotza chatichat ugat tapuchim?" Deena said to me. "Want a slice of apple cake?" Those were the only words that came out of her mouth toward me the whole day. In fact, she didn't even look at me when she said them.

It was like, it was like - oh, I don't care what it was like. It was like a hammer banging on my head, okay? Maybe there are worse things than people pretending to whisper about you. It's being invisible.

BBRRRINGGGG!!

Fire drill! We all had to go outside fast. We didn't even
have time to grab our coats! A real fire drill, like in
a regular school. So we rushed outside. Aviva and
Miri and Deena were all linking arms together in the
backyard to stay warm. (Chedva was sick that day.)

I tried to join in the circle, too, right between Miri
and Deena. But Deena locked her arms so hard
with Miri that I couldn't get in. They were like a big
human wall.

Maybe I should've just walked away. Instead I tried to
stick myself right between Miri and Aviva. But then
Deena hissed, "Lock your arms; don't let her in."

I looked at them. My heart knocked against my
chest. My toes went ice cold in my boots. Were
they going to listen to her? Were they? They
wouldn't look at me - not Aviva or Miri - and then

all three of them made a wall with their bodies and wouldn't let me in.

I closed my eyes a second. My throat felt clogged, like I'd swallowed a sock or something. Then I just walked away and stood next to Morah Zeldy. She was talking to Mrs. Berman. I don't think either of them saw a thing. As usual. Then Morah Zeldy put a hand on my shoulder. "Why aren't you standing with the other girls?" she asked in her friendly way.

I shrugged.

Mrs. Berman stared hard at me. Her eyes just locked onto mine. I felt a tiny tear coming to the corner of my eye, and I knew if I looked at her a second longer, a whole flood of tears would come out. Here Miri and Aviva had turned me away. And I thought they were my friends.

Morah Zeldy was watching the two of us, sort of squinting and trying to figure out what was going on. The strange thing was, Mrs. Berman's face suddenly looked sadder than mine. She looked as if her heart broke.

"I think I know why Bina's standing alone," she said quietly. She crossed her arms over her stomach like it was hurting her.

I'd never seen a mother look like that before. At least not my mother. And it hit me. Mrs. Berman had seen what happened. And that's what a mother looks like when she finds out her own daughter is mean. Really mean.

Today, when I came home, Ima asked me how school
was. I just went straight to my room, wouldn't say
a word or eat supper. Later, Ima and Abba were
so worried, they made me tell what had happened,
and bit by bit I told them about the fire drill.
Then I felt bad because I'd said lashon hara, but
Abba explained that if someone is bullying you at
school, it's a mitzvah to tell your parents, and not
an aveira. Ima got redder and redder in the face.
Then she tightened her mouth hard like when she
decides something, and nothing, I mean nothing, will
change her mind. She said, "She's not going back
to that school. I don't care if I have to bring all my
courtroom work home with me."

But Abba said, "You have a job, and I have a job,
and Bina has a job." He pointed at me. "It's going to
school. Even when it's not so pleasant."

Ima said loudly, "Not pleasant?" Pink splotches
popped out on her cheeks. "How can she go to a
school where every single girl in her class excludes
her?"

I threw in, "They were so mean to me. I hate them all."

Abba and Ima both said together, "Don't say 'hate.'"

Then Abba said, "It's our job - and the teacher's - to make the school a safe place for her until she starts her new school."

Ima stared at Abba and Abba stared back. Finally Ima said, "All right. After the school deals with this issue - properly - then Bina returns."

Malka came into the living room where we'd been talking. "Can I eat this?" She held up a cookie.

Ima nodded, distracted.

"It's not fair," Malka said between munches. "Bina doesn't have to go to school. So if my friends hate me, can I also stay home?"

I can't believe it. I guess I'm not the only snoop in this house. "Malka heard the whole thing!" I screeched.

Malka put her hand on my wrist. "Don't worry, Bina. If you don't have any friends, I'll let you play with mine."

The whole time I'd been listening to my parents talk, I'd stayed calm, but when Malka said that – I don't know – all the tears I'd been holding back started pushing their way out. I mean what could be worse than your little sister feeling sorry for you?

I couldn't stop blubbering. Then I caught a peek of myself in the hall mirror. I looked really horrible, my whole face one big cholent of blotchy skin and tears and I needed to blow my nose.

Whatever.

Malka tried to hug me. So did everybody. They were just trying to help me, right? But I pushed them all away and ran upstairs.

Question for the day: How come whenever I say "whatever," it doesn't feel like "whatever" and it still hurts so bad?

MOTZA'EI SHABBOS

Last night was Shabbos.

Ima said, "Don't think about everything today. Just enjoy Shabbos."

At first it was so hard. I couldn't stop thinking about what was bothering me. How my life has so many problems in it. More problems than normal.

"My life isn't normal," I said to Ima. "I'm not normal."

Ima said, "The only people who are normal are the ones you don't know so well."

I think that's true.

While Abba was at shul, Ima called me, Malka, and Levi into the living room to daven kabbalas Shabbos. Ima used to do that with us all the time, before she got so busy with her job. We thought it was so nice and special. But then since she started working so hard, after candlelighting she would just conk out in the

big easy chair and read one of the mothers' frum
magazines. But now we sat close to each other and
we sang Lecha Dodi, and it sounded so beautiful.
Just at that moment when we bowed and sang out,
"Bo'ee Kallah," I could almost feel an extra neshamah
flying down inside of me.

Later, I told that to Ima but to no one else, not
even Malka, because anyone else might think it's
weird. Not Ima, though. She hugged me and said,
"Me, too."

Ima made my favorite Shabbos soup, mushroom,
and my favorite kugel, pineapple. Everyone was
acting nicer.

Then guess what happened the next day?

Shaindy stopped by in the afternoon and we played
Perpetual Commotion and I told her about her
school becoming nut-free and that I'd probably be
going there next year. She jumped up, so excited
that her blond curls went boinging everywhere. "We

can walk to school together every day!"

"Yeah!" Then I added, "Maybe we'll be in the same class, too."

She shook her head. "They never put girls from the same block in the same class. It causes too many problems."

"What do you mean?"

"Well," Shaindy's head tilted like it did when she was thinking hard, "there's so many girls who are best friends from the same the block, but when they go to school and they're in the same class, suddenly they become enemies."

"Really?" I sat up straighter. "Why?"

"They just start to compete about everything. Who gets the best grades, who has the best snacks, or even best socks. Who can jump rope better. Anything."

I shifted in my chair. It reminded me of what was going on in my school. Sort of. But Deena and I don't live on the same block. "I wonder why living on the same block would make two girls hate each other."

"It's simple." Shaindy tossed one of her blond curls. "It's because they spend too much time with each other."

Wow. That really made me stop and think. Deena and I didn't live on the same block but it was just like that, or maybe even more, that's how much time we spent together. Maybe Deena and I had gotten too involved with each other, you know what I mean? Together too much. Competing, just like Shaindy said.

But before that idea could sink into my brain, I shook my head. No way. Deena's the one who's always been competing with ME and trying to boss ME, and not the other way around. I think she'd like to boss the whole world around, too, if she could.

Anyway, I got all excited, thinking of the fun
things Shaindy and I could do together - maybe
go to camp or take an art class together, but
then I started thinking, What if Shaindy turns
into another Deena? It could happen. Some days
she'll walk home with me; some days she'll decide
to walk home with that Blond Ponytail girl with
the bumpless hair. Or Shaindy might feel ashamed
of me, because I come from a different school
or because I'm different with my peanut allergy.
Shaindy could end up making my life miserable,
too.

Yeah, I know. I know all of that. But at least I
wouldn't be stuck having just four girls to choose
from. And if things got really bad, I could always
switch classes.

After Shaindy went home, I thought about that
whole competing thing again. I just couldn't stop
thinking about it. And I wondered, Could it be that
I'd been competing with Deena - just a little bit?
Like, maybe over Chedva? I blush just thinking

about it. Because I can get pretty competitive and
stubborn myself.

After Shabbos, I heard Ima talking on the phone.
She doesn't say any names, but I know who she's
talking to. Deena's mother.

Ima's voice sounds stiff and careful. I wish I could
hear what she was saying, but Ima doesn't let me
even get close.

After Ima gets off the phone, she has a half-smile,
half-frown on her face. "Interesting," Ima tells Abba
later on, when they're putting away the Havdalah
candle and spices and things. "She said now she
realizes things were more complicated between
the girls than she knew."

Still, I don't want to go back. And Ima and Abba
aren't making me until things get straightened out.
Not until it feels safe for me, they say.

Question for the day: What does "safe" even

mean? All I know is, when it's Shabbos I feel safe.

SUNDAY

I'm playing Pick-up Sticks with Levi while Ima is working on the computer. I'm sort of babysitting. So there's a knock on the door. I peer through the window to see who it is. Ima doesn't like it when I open the door to strangers. My mouth drops open. It's Morah Zeldy standing there on the front porch.

Without thinking, I open the door.

Her coat is a little open and I can see she's wearing

the blue dress with the fat buttons.

I'm so confused. For two reasons. Why is my teacher at my house, and why is she wearing her Monday outfit on a Sunday?

I just stand there staring at her until Morah Zeldy says, "So, Bina, are you going to let me in?"

I blush. "Of course." I pause. "I'll get my mother."

She holds up her palm. "Wait, I wanted to talk to you first, if that's okay."

I nod. I get a queasy feeling in my stomach. I just know what she's going to say. She's going to ask me to come back to school. And because she's a grown-up and my teacher, and I like her so much, I'll feel like I have to say yes. My stomach starts to hurt, like when I eat too much cholent on Shabbos.

Levi is still on the floor playing Pick-up Sticks. "Should I send my brother away?"

Morah Zelday slips out of her coat. "I don't mind if
he stays, as long as you don't mind."

Levi's concentrating real hard on those Pick-up
Sticks. I shrug. "It's okay."

Then I go to get her a drink. I don't even need to
ask what she likes. I know: plain water.

She thanks me, makes a slow bracha, and takes
a sip. Her fingers wrap around the cup when she
finishes. She opens her mouth as if she's about to
say something, and then she just coughs. I can't
believe it, but it seems like she's sort of nervous.
Well, just a little.

"I have something for you," she says finally.

"Really?"

"Something from the girls that they wrote."

"Oh." I don't know what to think. Actually, I do. Morah

Zeldy probably forced them all to write I'm Sorry and We Miss You letters. Who needs those lousy letters? Not me. Then I say, "All of the girls wrote?"

"I don't know who wrote and who didn't," Morah Zeldy says. "You'll have to see."

That makes me feel better a little. Maybe it means Morah Zeldy didn't force anyone to write them, then.

I hold out my hand for the letters, but she says, "Wait."

My arm drops.

"There's something I need to tell you." Morah Zeldy looks down at her hands for a long time, then she looks straight at me. "I really messed up," she says.

Huh? I blink at her. "What do you mean?"

"I mean," she says slowly, "I didn't do my job. I should've noticed things weren't right in the classroom."

I don't know what to say. Morah Zeldy's apologizing
- to me. I'm embarrassed. I just stare at the big
buttons on her blue dress. I almost mumble, "It
wasn't that bad," but I can't say that. It's not true.

Morah Zeldy lets out a very long sigh. "I found out
more about what went on. I wasn't keeping my eye
on things enough." She shakes her head a little.
"You know, kids can be sneaky," she says finally.
"They can do mean things and say mean things,
but they're careful to do it when the teacher isn't
around or can't hear them."

I nod, up and down. That's right, I think. Exactly.

Morah Zeldy sits up. "A teacher has to always be on
the lookout, to notice when things don't feel right.
During lunch or at recess or when the girls think she's
not around. She almost has to be ..." Again she pauses.

"A spy!" I jump in, and Morah Zeldy says, "Exactly,"
and gives me a how-did-you-know look.

I stare down at my shoes. That's right, I think. I'm feeling sad for Morah Zeldy, who is such a great teacher but she figured this out too late, and I'm feeling sad for me because I'm the one the girls were mean to and nobody paid attention, and then, suddenly, I don't feel so so sad anymore.

"Could I see those letters?" I ask.

She hands them over to me. I count them. Three in all.

The first one's from Aviva.

> To Bina Lobell,
> I am extremely annoyed that you're not in our class anymore. There is no one willing to listen to my talks about spiders and raisins and rabbits, and whatever important information comes to me. What am I going to do without you? I am awaiting your return.
> Sincerely, Aviva
> P.S. I was a real idiot for not including you the other day when we had the fire drill and I'm too

embarrassed to even talk about it. Sometimes I
act like an idiot, you know?

I smile. What an Aviva letter, you know what I mean?
So different from anybody I ever met. I kind of miss
her and all those talks of hers. She's so smart.

The next letter is Miri's.

Dear Bina,
You were the nicest, bestest thing about going
to school. I like you so so much. I feel so bad
if I ever did anything NOT NICE and hurt your
feelings. Please come back. Please come back.
Love,
Your friend Miri

I smile a little harder. I miss Miri more than I realized.
She's shy, but she has so much to say when you
talk to her, when it's just you and her and nobody
else is around.

Then, my hands shaking a little, I open one more

letter. Who is it from? Chedva or Deena? And who do I want it be from more?

I stare down. It's from Chedva. I remember how once I wanted to be her friend so bad and I thought she was such a tzaddekes. But now I don't feel anything. Just sort of empty inside. I slowly start to read.

Dear Bina,

I remember the first time I met you, and you were throwing a ball and catching it and humming at the same time and you had this little smile on your face, and I thought: That girl, I want her to be my friend. But somehow I was always too shy to make you my friend. Because the truth is, I have another big problem besides asthma. I get very shy and sort of scared around other girls, so I need to be in a small school and with girls younger than me, to make me feel more confident. I don't know why I'm telling you all this but I'll explode if I don't. So when you called me for that play date I was

so happy, remember? But somehow Deena
started paying a lot of attention to me at
the same time, and I got pulled to her side,
even though I didn't want there to be any sides
at all. And ever since then, it's like I'm all mixed
up and sad, even when I'm laughing and saying
'Watermelon.' At home I look at myself in the
mirror and say, "Chedva, is that really you? A
mean girl? A snobby girl?" And I have to say yes.
That's who I am - but I don't want to be that
way! I want to be your friend, your real friend.
I don't know if you'll come back to school or not,
but could I come over this Shabbos? Because I
really want to come.

Love,

Your friend Chedva, who wants to apologize but
doesn't know how

I put down the letter. I feel my eyes tearing up and I
blink hard and make the tears disappear.

I don't feel empty inside anymore. I feel full, like a
beanbag. Like I'm so happy to be me again.

I think about what Abba once told me about switching places with Shaindy or anybody. And how I didn't want to do that because then I wouldn't be me anymore. You know, I wouldn't have the funny, interesting parts and the parts that really care about my friends, the parts that make me Bina. Just then this crazy idea pops into my head – Could it be my allergy helped make me that way? Different in a good way? Maybe my allergy gave me a lot of good stuff, too, not just the hard-to-deal-with stuff. This idea surprises me so much I almost forget Morah Zeldy is right there staring at me, waiting for me to say something.

So I ask her, "Where's the last letter?"

She spreads out her hands.

Nothing from Deena. Of course. She doesn't think she did anything wrong. I look up and see Morah Zeldy staring at me, like she's trying to guess what I'm thinking. She probably thinks I'm a baby. Like, if I didn't get a letter from everybody, then

I won't go back. Actually, that's exactly what I'm thinking.

But you know what? I'll fool her. I'll fool everybody. I'll go back. Not for good, but just to finish fourth grade with my class. Because they really are my friends - well, most of them - even if they got influenced and acted mean toward the end. And then I'll go to Bnos Devora.

I tell this to Morah Zeldy and she nods and smiles at me. "Very good decision," she says, and for the first time in weeks, I feel normal and okay inside.

Levi says, "Yay, Bina" and throws his Pick-up Sticks in the air.

Ima comes up from the basement and

I tell her that tomorrow I'll be going back to school. I wish I'd taken a picture, just to capture the look of shock on her face. Happy shock, you know what I mean?

Just before I go to sleep, though, I think what it will be like tomorrow. I know it'll be a great day with everyone crowding around me and making me feel good. I just know it. Then Deena will be the one left out of the circle.

Of course, I'll say, "Hi Deena," and talk to her and make her feel good, not left out or anything. But before I do that, I'll wait a minute, so that she'll know - even if it's just for a minute - what it feels like to be left out.

Then I say Shema and shut the lights.

Question for the day: When a girl turns mean, and I'm talking really, really mean, can she ever really turn nice again?

MONDAY

Everything's back to the same - the same, but really sooo different.

Yep, I went back to school today. As soon as I stepped inside I saw a big fruit salad - my favorite - on the work table, and a huge sign on the wall that said, "Welcome Back, Bina! We Love You!"

Miri, who was standing near the glass beakers, rushed up and hugged me. Aviva ran up, too, holding a whole box of spiders, shoving it under my nose.

"Isn't this cool?" she kept saying.

I peered inside, then looked away. "Cool," I said. The cool part was being back at school with friends again.

I looked around. There was Chedva sort of shuffling her feet, looking like she didn't know what to do, so I just said, "Hey, Chedva."

The biggest, shiniest smile took over her whole face. "Hi, Bina!" she practically yelled. Then she came and gave me a big hug, too.

Next thing I knew, all three girls had joined hands and started dancing around me. But I felt strange being in the middle, so I joined the circle.

And there was Deena off to the side, pretending to be into her "work." You know, crocheting or knitting something - looking kind of bored. And, I know I said I would leave her out for a minute, just so she would feel how I felt. But seeing her there, I couldn't ... I just couldn't. That would be nekamah, pure revenge. So I say, "Hey, Deena," because I can tell she's just pretending to be bored, you know?

When I say "Hey," she looks up real fast and says, "I want to show you something I made!"

I'm about to run over to her like I always used to do whenever Deena called me, but then I stop myself. I say, "I really want to see it. Can you come here and show us?"

That old Deena look comes over her face, like Don't-you-tell-me-what-to-do ... But then she slips off her seat and comes toward us. She holds up this crocheted sign. It says, "Aviva, Bina, Chedva, Deena, Miri - Best Friends 4ever!"

She made it out of yellow and purple threads, with a little green trimming, and it's gorgeous. "Wow, Deena!" I breathe out.

"You listed the names in alphabetical order," Chedva comments.

"So there wouldn't be any fighting," Deena explains.

I touch it. The letters look so perfect. I feel so sad/happy. Best friends 4ever. Could it happen? Could I ever trust Deena?

"Morah Zeldy," I call out. "Could we hang this sign up? Please?"

Morah Zeldy takes the sign into her hands, holds it up, admires it. "Of course. Let's hang it over the netillas yadayim sink. That way you'll see it just before you go to eat lunch every day."

So that's what we do.

Afterwards, Morah Zeldy gives a talk about how we all need to be looking out for each other, and if someone isn't getting treated right, we need to stand up and say something, to be brave. Even if it's just to say, "It's not okay to leave out Bracha when you jump rope," or "Don't make fun of Leah's lunch," or "Stop whispering behind someone's back - it's mean." She said that to be a real Torahdik Jew, you need to be brave, like Queen Esther, like Avraham, like all the avos and imahos, to stand up for what's right. And you also need to be brave, to stick up for your own self.

Tzaddekeses
in Training

Morah Zeldy gets more excited as she talks, her
eyes getting sharp and like full of fire, and her
arms waving all over the place, like she wants to fix
the whole wide world, but then she stops suddenly,
folds her arms, and looks like the regular Morah
Zeldy we know, and says, "Girls, time for lunch."

At lunch, we all eat our food together, and it
doesn't even bother me that Aviva's tuna fish
smells so strong. We're laughing and having fun like
we used to, when suddenly I realize Miri and Chedva

and Aviva got up to go somewhere and it's just me and Deena sitting at the table.

She looks at me and I look at her. My heart starts pounding so loud I can feel it in my ears and throat, sort of.

There's a quiet between us. A very very loud quiet. One of us has to speak. Just has to. Because how can I pretend everything's normal if we never even talked about what happened?

"Why did you start hating me so much?"

I can't believe I said that out loud.

Deena blinks. Her face goes kind of pale. She stops chewing her sandwich.

I think she's going to say I never hated you! but then she shrugs and says, "I don't know. It just kind of happened. Out of nowhere."

At first I feel relieved, because I was sure all along that she hated me, but I kept telling myself, How could that be, a best friend who hates you? So at least I know now that I wasn't crazy. I was right. But now I start to get mad. I mean, what did I ever do to make her hate me?

So I ask her.

Deena pulls her fingers like she always does when she doesn't know the answer. "I got jealous, I guess." She stares at the table as she says this. Won't look at me.

I don't say anything.

Deena slouches in her seat. "I just started thinking all kinds of things. One minute we were best friends, but then Morah Zeldy complimented you on your project and I didn't like it that yours was better than mine. It made me mad. And then I thought you were going around trying to get everyone to like you and hate me, so I figured I should start doing the same and get them to hate you first."

I shake my head a little. How could she be so mean?

Then I think of the way I attacked Malka because of the socks, and Levi when he played with my stamps. And how easy it is to forget how much I love them and how when I'm angry, nothing in the world can stop me. I can be mean, too. Plenty mean.

Deena says in a quiet voice, "I'm sorry." I look at her, sitting there, slouching, her hair sort of falling into her eyes. I feel bad for her, but then I think: Sure she looks sad and sorry now, but what about tomorrow? You know what I think? She'll always be a not-easy friend, the friend who tries to boss you around, tell you what to do, mess up the hair of your favorite doll. She'll always be Deena. Just then, though, a new thought hits me: So what? Why can't I still have fun with her sometimes? Sure I can! Because when she tries to boss me around, this

time I won't let her. Besides, we'll be in different
schools next year, so we won't be seeing each
other so much.

Deena is waiting for me to speak. She peeps at
me and then I peep back at her, to let her know
everything's okay between us, and we both break
into big smiles.

Deena sits up and brushes the hair off her face.
"Guess what? My mother's now saying she doesn't
think the Monty Sorry homeschool is the best
place for me. She's thinking of sending me to a
regular school. I can't wait!"

Then Morah Zeldy announces lunch is over and we
clean up and all go back to our work places.

Question for the day: What if - gulp - Deena
follows me to my new school?

Whatever.

GLOSSARY

Abba - Daddy

Amen - response to a
blessing

Amos - cubits; a cubit is
about 1.5-2 feet

Ashrei - Psalm 145

Aveira - sin

Avos - forefathers

Avraham - Abraham, our
forefather

Bo'ee Kallah - the last part of
Lecha Dodi, a song sung on
Friday night

Bracha - blessing

Challah - traditional braided
bread eaten on the
Sabbath and holidays

Chanukah - holiday that
celebrates the victory of
the Jews over the Seleucid
Greeks during the Second
Temple era

Chesed - act of kindness

Chol HaMoed - intermediate
days of the holidays of
Passover and Sukkos

Cholent - traditional stew
eaten on the Sabbath

Chutzpah - disrespect

Chutzpahdik - being
disrespectful

Daven - pray

Esrog - citron, one of the
Four Species used on the
holiday of Sukkos

Hachnasas orchim -
welcoming guests

Hashem - the Almighty

Havdalah - blessing made at
the end of the Sabbath

Ima - Mommy

Imahos - foremothers

Kabbalas Shabbos - prayers
recited on Friday night to

welcome the Sabbath

Kallah - bride

Kiddush Hashem -

   sanctification of the

   Almighty's name

Kugel - baked pudding

Lashon hara - gossip

Lecha Dodi - song sung on

   Friday night to welcome

   the Sabbath

Lulav - palm branch, one of

   the Four Species used on

   the holiday of Sukkos

Melachos - activities

   forbidden on the Sabbath

Middos - character traits

Mitzvah - Torah

   commandment

Modeh Ani - prayer of thanks

   recited upon waking up in

   the morning

Motza'ei Shabbos -

   Saturday night

Neshama - soul

Netilas yadayim -

   ritual hand washing

Pushka - charity box

Queen Esther - heroine of

   the Purim story

Rebbetzin - rabbi's wife

Rosh Chodesh -

   the New Moon

Shabbos - the Sabbath

Shaitel - wig

Shalom - peace

Shalosh Seudos - third meal

   of the Sabbath

Shema - prayer that

   proclaims the unity of the

   Almighty

Shemoneh Esrei - main Jewish

   prayer

Shul - synagogue

Sukkos - holiday that

   commemorates how the

   Almighty protected the

Jews in the desert for

forty years

Tallis - prayer shawl

Tehillim - Psalms

Teivah - Noah's ark

Torah - the Bible

Tzadekkes - righteous woman

Yaakov - Jacob, our

forefather

Yerushalayim - Jerusalem

Yetzer hara - evil inclination

Yishtabach - blessing ending

the prayer section called

Pesukei D'zimra

Yom Kippur - the Day of

Atonement